In a world where deception often seems to win and doing the right thing can feel like a losing battle, it's easy to grow tired. To stay silent. To let bitterness harden what used to be tender.

But I believe in something better.

This story is a reminder that integrity still matters—even when it costs more than we ever thought we'd have to give. That telling the truth, standing firm, and loving people—even broken ones—isn't weakness. It's courage. It's obedience. It's the reflection of a God who never lies, never manipulates, and never turns away from justice or mercy.

Living with integrity is not easy. Especially now. But it's still worth it.

With love and conviction,

Stephanie Olds

Stephanie Olds

THIRTY
PIECES

TABLE OF CONTENTS

PROLOGUE

THE JUDAS KISS OF TRUST

"For it is not an enemy who taunts me—then I could bear it; it is not an adversary who deals insolently with me—then I could hide from him. But it is you, a man my equal, my companion, my familiar friend."
—Psalm 55:12-13 (ESV)

The judge's voice was a distant hum, drowned out by the weight of what she had lost. There are moments in life that divide everything into 'before' and 'after.' This was her after.

Celeste sat motionless at the long mahogany table, her hands folded tightly in her lap. The air in the courtroom was stale, thick with the scent of old paper, polished wood, and something faintly metallic—perhaps the weight of consequence itself. The leather chair beneath her felt stiff, unyielding, as if it too had decided to turn against her.

The judge spoke, words tumbling into the cavernous room, but Celeste barely processed them. She had heard enough legal jargon in the past three years to last a lifetime. *Motion denied. Case dismissed. The plaintiff assumes all legal fees.* The phrases blurred together, sharp but meaningless. None of it mattered now.

What mattered was the finality of it all.

Three hundred thousand dollars. Gone. Not stolen. Not misplaced. Spent—because she had trusted the wrong person.

A shuffling sound broke through her daze—her attorney shifting beside her, stacking papers that no longer served a purpose. He murmured something, but Celeste couldn't bring herself to respond. Instead, she let her gaze wander through the room, scanning faces that seemed so distant, so unfamiliar.

Valerie's seat was empty for the moment. Celeste could almost feel her absence, like a heavy presence lingering over her shoulder.

A slow, nauseating realization twisted in Celeste's gut.

It had never been about justice. It had never been about truth.

It had always been about keeping a secret.

Her grandmother used to say that deception was like a Judas kiss—*looks like love, feels like love, but delivers ruin instead.* Celeste had never fully understood that before.

A sharp sting burned behind her eyes, but she refused to blink. She wouldn't cry. Not here. Not now.

Instead, she exhaled, slow and measured, pressing her nails into her palm until pain grounded her. She reached for the documents in front of her, ran her fingertips over the embossed seal of the court.

Final. Official. Done.

And so was she.

She pushed her chair back, the scrape of wood against tile louder than she intended, and rose to her feet. The weight of the room seemed to follow her with every step.

As she crossed the threshold, one thought settled in her mind with chilling certainty.

Some betrayals cost more than money.

———

CHAPTER ONE

STRATEGIC PARTNERSHIPS

"A single lie discovered is enough to create doubt in every truth expressed."
—Unknown

Celeste Monroe stepped out of her sleek, black Audi and into the warm morning air, taking a deep breath before striding toward the towering glass office building. The sound of her heels against the pavement was crisp, confident. She adjusted the fitted blazer of her navy-blue pantsuit and smoothed a hand over her silk blouse—presentation mattered, always.

Growing up, there were no handouts, which instilled in her a strong sense of self-reliance and determination. Holding a master's degree in business administration made her a respected force in the corporate world. For her, it wasn't just about the money—though she was more than comfortable—it was about competence, control, and excellence. She had never cut corners, never taken the easy way, and never asked for a handout.

Celeste had spent her childhood in a cramped three-bedroom house, sharing a tiny room with three siblings. Space was limited. Privacy was nonexistent. Clothes were passed down until the fabric thinned. She learned early on that if she wanted something new, she'd have to earn it herself.

While other kids got brand-new backpacks and the latest sneakers, Celeste had thrift store finds and clearance rack specials. But what she lacked in material things, she made up for in intellect. She was the kind of student teachers didn't forget—the one who sat in the front, asked the hard questions, and turned in extra credit work even when she had a perfect score.

At every level, she was a standout. Not because she was naturally gifted, but because she refused to be outworked.

When it came time for college, she didn't just want an education—she wanted an HBCU experience. She wanted to be surrounded by Black excellence, to learn from professors who saw her potential before she saw it in herself. She chose an HBCU with one of the toughest business programs in the country and graduated with high honors.

Every degree, every promotion, every success—she had fought for it. Her journey was marked by late nights and early mornings, fueled by an unyielding determination and a vision that never wavered. At 35 years old, she had everything she had worked for and had built a life exactly how she wanted it, from the ground up. A 3,200-square-foot home inside an exclusive gated community, where every room echoed with the stories of her triumphs. A career where she wasn't just present—she was a trailblazer, setting new standards and inspiring those around her to reach for more. Her leadership style was both compassionate and firm, earning her the admiration of her peers and the loyalty of her team.

Her achievements extended beyond the corporate world. She was a sought-after speaker at industry conferences, where her insights were not just heard but revered. Her name appeared in prestigious business magazines, highlighting her as one of the top influencers in her field. She had authored a best-selling book on leadership, sharing her journey and the principles that guided her success.

A paid-off luxury car, a fully funded investment portfolio, and the financial freedom to take care of herself on her terms were just the beginning. She had also established a charitable foundation, channeling her blessings into opportunities for others, embodying the love and grace she believed in. Her life was a testament to the power of hard work and faith, and she lived it unapologetically.

She had earned all of it. And if there was one thing she refused to tolerate, it was people who mistook privilege for effort. Her amazing qualities made others uncomfortable, and some even hated her for it, but she knew that was their burden to bear, not hers. She was beyond blessed, and she carried that blessing with humility and strength, knowing that her journey was far from over.

Stepping inside the building, she was greeted with the scent of fresh coffee and polished marble. The company was a major player in logistics and supply chain management, and Celeste had carved her niche in strategic planning and business analytics. She was the one executives turned to when they needed results. She was the fixer, the problem solver. And she had earned every ounce of respect in this place.

As she approached the executive elevators, a familiar voice called out.

"Celeste! Hey, girl!"

She turned, smiling as Valerie Henshaw made her way over, her heels clicking just a little too fast, as if she were rushing to catch up. Valerie was ten years older, but something about her energy felt... slightly strained. She had the kind of smile that could be warm but never quite reached her eyes. Her clothes were expensive but never quite tailored.

Celeste waited as Valerie caught up, tucking a strand of her shoulder-length brown hair behind her ear.

"You are a vision, as always," Valerie said, eyeing Celeste's outfit with something that wasn't quite jealousy—but close. *"I swear, you make me feel like a damn soccer mom."*

Celeste let out a soft laugh. *"You say that like it's a bad thing."*

Valerie rolled her eyes. *"It is when I don't even like soccer. Or being a mom half the time."* She sighed, then lowered her voice. *"Nathan was up all night with some stomach bug. I barely got three hours of sleep."*

Celeste gave a sympathetic nod, but it wasn't the first time she had heard something like this. Valerie often spoke about her home life with a tinge of exhaustion, an undertone of regret.

"I don't know how you do it, Celeste." Valerie shook her head. *"You've got your dream house, your dream job. No husband, no kids—just you, doing you. That's the life."*

Celeste smiled, but there was something sharp beneath it. She had always wanted a family. She just hadn't found the right man, and she refused to settle for less than what she deserved. But explaining that to someone like Valerie? Not worth it.

Instead, she kept it simple. *"It's not as glamorous as you think."*

"Please," Valerie scoffed. *"You don't have to deal with a husband who thinks 'helping' means microwaving frozen pizza, or a kid who whines every time I ask her to clean her room."*

Celeste didn't respond right away. Valerie had a way of making motherhood and marriage sound like a prison sentence. It was strange. Weren't those things supposed to be a blessing?

The elevator doors opened, and they stepped inside. As the doors slid shut, Valerie glanced at Celeste.

"Honestly, you don't know how good you have it."

For a moment, Celeste almost laughed. Good? Sure. She had worked damn hard for what she had. No one handed her a six-figure salary. No one gave her a blueprint for success. She made sacrifices. She put in the work.

And yet, as she glanced at Valerie, she couldn't shake the feeling that somehow... Valerie resented her for it.

―――――

Celeste was halfway through her lunch when her phone buzzed.

Valerie Henshaw Calling...

She wiped her hands, picked up, and barely got out a greeting before Valerie's voice filled the line.

"Ugh. I swear, this job is going to kill me."

Celeste smirked, leaning back in her chair. *"What did they do this time?"*

"Oh, you know. The usual corporate nonsense. Do everything, solve everything, and still get ignored when it's time for promotions." Valerie sighed dramatically. *"I don't know how you put up with this place."*

Celeste chuckled. *"Because I don't wait for promotions. I make myself impossible to overlook."*

Silence. Just for a second. Then—

"See, that's what I mean," Valerie said. *"You always know how to position yourself. How do you do that?"*

Celeste blinked. *"I don't know. I just—make myself valuable."*

"No, no." Valerie's tone was serious now. *"Like, when you speak in meetings? People listen. You could say the same thing I do, and somehow, it lands better coming from you. I swear, you have a gift."*

Celeste laughed, but the compliment felt… heavier than usual.

"It's not a gift, Val. It's just strategy."

"Exactly." Valerie paused. *"Would you help me with that?"*

Celeste frowned. *"Help you how?"*

*"I don't know. Give me pointers. You have this confidence, this **presence**. I could use some of that."*

Celeste tilted her head, considering. Valerie was ten years older, had more experience, and yet—she was asking *her* for help?

It felt… backwards.

But Celeste didn't hesitate. *"Of course. Anything you need."*

––––––

Celeste stood at the large conference table, adjusting the papers in front of her. The glass walls of the executive boardroom reflected the dim evening light, and most of the office had already emptied out for the day.

She checked her watch—6:47 PM.

The meeting had ended nearly an hour ago, but she and Valerie had stayed behind. It wasn't unusual. These post-meeting breakdowns had become a habit over the past few years— Celeste dissecting what had gone well, what could have been better, and Valerie offering insight.

"You did good in there," Valerie said, leaning against the table with her arms crossed. *"You had that supply chain guy in the palm of your hand."*

Celeste smirked, slipping her notes into a folder. *"He wasn't that difficult. Just needed the numbers framed in a way that made sense to him."*

Valerie nodded approvingly. *"See? That's the difference between you and most people in this building."*

Celeste tilted her head. *"How so?"*

Valerie pushed away from the table and started pacing slowly. *"Most people just do their job. You? You control the room."* She gestured toward the empty seats. *"You make people want to agree with you. That's why you're going places."*

Celeste felt warmth spread in her chest. Compliments from Valerie always carried extra weight.

Valerie had been the first senior-level woman Celeste had truly admired when she joined the company. She had experience, confidence, a directness that Celeste respected. In the beginning, Celeste had absorbed everything Valerie had to offer—her strategic thinking, her ability to command a conversation, her sharp way of cutting through corporate nonsense.

For a while, Celeste had thought of Valerie as a mentor.

Maybe she still did.

"I learned from the best," Celeste said, giving Valerie a knowing look.

Valerie chuckled. *"Don't blame me when you start making enemies."*

Celeste rolled her eyes. *"I don't care about making friends. I care about results."*

Valerie stopped pacing and studied her, a slow smile forming. *"That's what I like about you."*

A comfortable silence settled between them, the hum of the empty office filling the air.

Then Valerie sighed, shifting slightly. *"You know... I used to be you."*

Celeste raised an eyebrow. *"What do you mean?"*

"Young. Ambitious. Sharp." Valerie's expression darkened slightly, her fingers tracing the edge of the table. *"I had big plans too. But then life happens. You get married. You have kids. You make... sacrifices."*

Celeste wasn't sure how to respond. Valerie sounded almost wistful. Almost bitter.

"I wouldn't change my life," Valerie added quickly, her smile returning—though it seemed a bit strained. *"But just know... it's not always as simple as climbing the ladder."*

Celeste observed her closely, a new thought flickering in her mind. Perhaps Valerie's admiration held a hint of something more complex.

It started with small things. Reviewing Valerie's reports before she submitted them. Helping her reword emails to sound more authoritative. Offering advice before big meetings.

Then it escalated.

Valerie would call late at night, frustrated about a situation at work. She started venting about leadership, about unfair treatment, about Celeste's *"natural advantage."*

"You're lucky, you know that?" she had said once. *"You don't have to fight to be taken seriously."*

Celeste had disagreed, but she didn't argue.

Then came the project collaborations.

Valerie started pushing for joint projects with Celeste, attaching herself to Celeste's work. The higher-ups noticed. And soon, Valerie was benefiting—getting credit, receiving praise, enjoying bonuses.

Celeste didn't mind, until it became clear that Valerie's intentions were not as straightforward as they seemed.

A year later, Celeste found herself sitting across from Valerie at their usual café, her spoon lazily tracing circles in her tea. The familiar clatter of cups and soft murmur of conversations filled the air, but her mind was elsewhere.

"Hey," Valerie chimed in, her voice bright as she took a leisurely sip of her latte. *"Did you happen to catch the new org chart?"*

Celeste glanced up, her curiosity piqued. *"Yeah, I noticed they added a new senior strategy role."*

Valerie leaned in slightly, her eyes sparkling with a mix of excitement and something else Celeste couldn't quite place. *"And guess who's stepping into those shoes?"*

Celeste blinked, her heart skipping a beat. *"You?"*

Valerie's grin was wide, almost too wide. *"Yours truly."*

A strange sensation settled in Celeste's stomach, a mix of pride and something more elusive. She should have been thrilled for Valerie. After all, Valerie had been eyeing this role for ages, and Celeste had been there every step of the way, offering guidance and support.

Yet, there was an unsettling feeling she couldn't shake. Valerie's ascent seemed rapid, almost as if propelled by an unseen force. Was it Valerie's own brilliance, or had Celeste's efforts played a larger role than she realized?

Still, she mustered a smile, pushing aside her doubts. *"Congratulations, Val."*

Valerie's eyes twinkled with a hint of mischief. *"Couldn't have done it without you."*

The words hung in the air, ostensibly a gesture of gratitude. But to Celeste, they felt layered, as if they carried a deeper meaning, a subtle acknowledgment of debts unpaid.

She nodded, her smile unwavering, even as her mind raced with questions she wasn't ready to confront.

CHAPTER TWO

WITNESS

"The eye sees only what the mind is prepared to comprehend."
— *Robertson Davies*

Celeste adjusted the strap of her handbag and stepped into the café, the scent of roasted espresso beans curling into the cool air around her. The place was familiar—warm lighting, soft chatter, the occasional clink of ceramic cups meeting saucers. She had been here dozens of times before but today felt different. Or maybe that was just her mind, already weighed down by the conversation she was about to have.

She spotted Valerie first, already seated near the back corner, her fingers wrapped around a steaming cup. Celeste weaved past occupied tables, nodding slightly at the barista who recognized her. She was a creature of habit—same café, same drink order, same predictable routines that gave her life a sense of stability.

Valerie looked up as she approached, her expression unreadable for the briefest moment before she forced a smile.

"There you are. I was starting to think you got lost."

Celeste slid into the chair across from her, setting her bag down before unbuttoning her coat. *"I had to take a call. Work's a mess today."*

Valerie scoffed. *"When is it not?"*

That was how their friendship had started—shared exhaustion, mutual exasperation, and an unshakable belief that their workplace was being driven into the ground by incompetence. Five years ago, they had met at a corporate training event, forced into the same breakout group under the ever-watchful eye of Hope—the logistics planning manager who, by all measures, should have been nowhere near logistics planning.

Hope was a disaster. Not in the entertaining, lovable way that made for good office gossip, but in the soul-crushing, work-derailing, how-does-she-still-have-a-job kind of way. She was consistently late on deliverables, disorganized to the point of absurdity, and so thin-skinned that any constructive criticism was met with tears or a strategic retreat into sick leave. If she made a mistake—and she often did—it was never her fault. Leadership, rather than addressing her failings, wrapped her in protective layers of excuses, coddling her as if she were the company's fragile, wayward child rather than an actual manager responsible for critical supply chain operations.

Celeste and Valerie had both been burned by her incompetence more times than they could count.

"She's got to go," Valerie had muttered to Celeste during one of the training exercises, watching Hope fumble through an explanation of inventory forecasting that was, at best, a work of creative fiction.

Celeste had raised an eyebrow. *"Oh, you think?"*

"I'm serious." Valerie leaned in, lowering her voice. *"We work too damn hard for people like her to make six figures failing upward. If I ever get to a place where I can make real decisions in this company, people like her? Gone."*

Celeste had smirked. *"Remind me to stay on your good side."*

"I don't take issue with people who do their jobs. Just the ones who don't."

That was the moment Celeste knew they were of the same mind. They both valued competence, accountability, and the belief that no one—*no one*—was entitled to power if they couldn't handle responsibility. Hope had become their cautionary tale, a symbol of everything wrong with leadership's willingness to protect the wrong people.

Now, five years later, Celeste still respected that about Valerie—her decisiveness, her unwillingness to tolerate nonsense. She might not have considered Valerie her best friend, but she trusted her judgment. She trusted that they saw the world the same way.

Valerie pushed a second cup of coffee toward her. *"Got yours. No sugar, extra shot."*

Celeste smirked. *"You do know me well."*

She took a sip, letting the bitterness settle on her tongue. For all their differences, Valerie had always been the type to pay attention. She remembered small details, anticipated what people needed before they said it. It was one of the reasons Celeste respected her—Valerie wasn't just smart, she was aware.

"I wasn't sure if we'd meet today," Celeste said after a pause. *"You seemed... off when you texted."*

Valerie let out a slow breath, her fingers tightening around her cup. *"Yeah. I just—I have something to tell you."*

Celeste raised an eyebrow, waiting.

Valerie swallowed, looking down at the table before speaking. *"I saw something. Something bad."*

Her voice was low, almost a whisper, and suddenly, the familiar café felt too open, too exposed.

Celeste leaned in slightly. *"What do you mean?"*

Valerie exhaled sharply, shaking her head. *"I don't even know how to explain it, Celeste. It's been eating at me, and I didn't know if I should say anything, but—"* She broke off, pressing a hand to her temple. *"I can't just stay quiet."*

A thin thread of unease wove through Celeste's ribs. *"Okay,"* she said slowly. *"Whatever it is, you can tell me."*

Valerie looked up then, eyes dark with something unreadable. Guilt? Fear?

"I witnessed something," she said finally. *"And I think I need to go to the police."*

Valerie's words hung between them, heavy and unresolved. Celeste felt her spine straighten instinctively. She had seen Valerie upset before—frustrated with work, stressed about home—but this was different. There was something raw in her voice, something that made Celeste's skin prickle with unease.

She set her coffee down carefully. *"Girl, tell me what happened."*

Valerie hesitated, fingers drumming against her cup, gaze flicking toward the door as if checking for eavesdroppers. Then, finally, she spoke.

"I was out late last night," she began, voice hushed. *"I couldn't sleep, so I went for a drive. Just needed to clear my head, you know?"*

Celeste nodded, though she had never been the type to go driving in the middle of the night.

"I ended up near that development over on Willow Creek—the new office spaces they're building." Valerie took a slow breath. *"And that's when I saw it."*

"Saw what?"

"A man," she said, lowering her voice even further. *"He was— he was breaking in, Celeste."*

Celeste blinked, absorbing the weight of those words. *"Breaking in?"*

"Yes. I saw him near the back entrance, messing with the lock. At first, I thought maybe I was wrong, maybe he worked there, but then—" She shook her head. *"Then he forced the door open. He forced it. And I just... I froze."*

Celeste frowned. *"You're sure?"*

Valerie's eyes flashed. *"I know what I saw."*

A slight edge had crept into her voice, and Celeste immediately regretted the question.

"I didn't know what to do," Valerie continued, looking down at her hands. *"I mean, I could've called the cops right then, but what if I was wrong? What if it was nothing? So I waited, just for a minute."* She swallowed hard. *"And then he came back out... carrying something."*

A pulse of unease ran through Celeste. *"What was it?"*

"I don't know. But it was small, like he was hiding it under his jacket." Valerie exhaled sharply. *"I should've called the police. I should've done something right then, but I just—Celeste, I panicked. And then he was gone."*

Celeste sat back, processing. A break-in. A stolen item. No police report.

She wasn't sure what unsettled her more—the crime itself or the way Valerie was looking at her, waiting, as if Celeste's response carried more weight than anything else.

"What do you think I should do?" Valerie finally asked.

Celeste's answer came without hesitation. *"You need to report it."*

Valerie let out a slow, uneven breath and rubbed her hands over her face. *"I don't know what to do, Celeste. I feel sick even talking about it."*

Celeste watched her carefully, taking in the tension in Valerie's shoulders, the way her fingers tapped restlessly against the ceramic cup. Valerie was a woman who prided herself on having everything under control. Seeing her like this—rattled, uncertain—made Celeste's stomach tighten.

"You're doing the right thing by telling me," Celeste said gently. *"And you knew what I was going to say. You need to report this."*

Valerie shook her head. *"It's not that simple."*

Celeste leaned forward slightly. *"Why not?"*

Valerie exhaled sharply. *"Because I don't even know exactly what was taken. What if it was nothing? What if I'm overreacting and I ruin someone's life over nothing?"*

"That's not your responsibility," Celeste countered. *"If there was a break-in, if you saw someone tampering with a locked building and taking something—someone needs to investigate. That's how this works."*

The server approached, setting down a small plate with a warmed cheese Danish in front of Celeste. *"Here you go,"* she said with a polite smile before walking away.

Celeste blinked in mild surprise. She hadn't expected anything besides coffee.

Valerie nudged the plate slightly toward her. *"I ordered it when I got here. Figured you wouldn't, but you always regret it when you don't."*

Despite the weight of their conversation, Celeste felt a flicker of appreciation. Valerie had a knack for being considerate in the tiniest details, always recalling people's preferences and foreseeing their needs. It was part of what made her such a natural leader.

She picked off a small piece of the pastry but hesitated before eating it. *"Have you told anyone else? Security? HR?"*

Valerie let out a humorless laugh. *"HR?"* She shook her head. *"You really think they'd care? HR exists to protect the company, not us."*

Celeste frowned but didn't disagree. HR had been useless when they'd raised concerns about Hope's incompetence—why would this be any different?

"And security?" Celeste pressed.

Valerie hesitated. *"I... don't know who to trust. What if someone in security is involved?"*

Celeste considered that. It wasn't impossible. If something shady was happening at one of the company's properties, who's to say it wasn't an inside job?

"I know you won't let this slide. I wanted you to be the first to know," Valerie said, her voice dropping to a conspiratorial whisper. *"I trust you, Celeste. You've always been the one to stand firm, to do what's right, no matter what."* Valerie's words hung in the air, a subtle acknowledgment of Celeste's unwavering principles.

Celeste sat back slightly, chewing over the weight of that statement.

"I can go with you," she said at last. *"To the police."*

Valerie let out a breath—relief, maybe—but there was something else behind it. Something almost imperceptible.

And just like that, Valerie had what she needed.

———————

Celeste arrived at the station five minutes before Valerie. She didn't like being late for anything, and besides, she needed a moment to collect her thoughts.

The scent of disinfectant and stale coffee lingered in the air as she pushed open the heavy glass doors of the precinct. Fluorescent lights buzzed faintly overhead, casting a dull glow over the gray walls and rows of chairs. She chose one near the entrance, its plastic surface cool and unyielding beneath her, her fingers drumming lightly against her thigh. Nearby, she noticed a few upholstered chairs, each a relic of countless waiting hours, their once-vibrant upholstery now faded and threadbare. They presumably offered a slightly more comfortable option for those who lingered longer in the lobby.

A large corkboard across from her was covered in flyers—missing persons, community alerts, and a yellowed poster with the words:

"IF YOU SEE SOMETHING, SAY SOMETHING."

It felt like a sign.

The station was busy but not chaotic—officers moved with purpose, taking reports, making calls, escorting handcuffed individuals to the back.

She took a deep breath, whispering a silent prayer. *"Lord, let the truth come to light."*

Before she could dwell on the thought, Valerie strode through the entrance, wrapped in a navy blazer that made her look effortlessly put together. Her expression was carefully curated—concerned, but not panicked. A woman with nothing to hide.

"*Ready?*" she asked, her voice steady.

Celeste nodded, standing. "*Yeah. Let's do this.*"

Valerie led the way, arms crossed tightly over her chest, eyes darting toward every passing officer.

"*Are you okay?*" Celeste asked, lowering her voice as they approached the front desk.

Valerie nodded quickly. "*Yeah. Just nervous.*"

The officer behind the desk glanced up, looking between them with mild interest. "*How can I help you ladies?*"

Valerie hesitated just long enough for Celeste to step forward.

"*We'd like to report a break-in,*" Celeste said firmly.

The officer sat up straighter, pulling out a form. "*Alright. Where and when?*"

Valerie exhaled and placed a hand on the counter.

"*It was at the new development on Willow Creek. Last night. Late.*"

He grabbed a notepad. "*Alright, and you are?*"

"Valerie Henshaw." She nudged Celeste lightly. *"And this is Celeste Monroe. She's my witness."*

Celeste blinked. Witness?

The word hit her with more weight than she expected.

The officer's gaze shifted to her, and he gave a slow nod. *"You witnessed it? You saw what happened?"*

There was a moment's hesitation—barely noticeable, but it was there. Celeste didn't *see* anything. She was going off what Valerie had told her. But still, she nodded. *"I have reason to believe that what Valerie saw was serious enough to investigate."*

Valerie nodded approvingly, placing a reassuring hand on Celeste's wrist, just for a second. A subtle move, but an effective one.

The officer scribbled something down. *"Alright. Let's get a full statement. Follow me."*

———————

Celeste followed Valerie and the officer down a short hallway to a small, windowless room lined with filing cabinets. A single table sat in the center, cluttered with papers and a few pens.

The officer gestured for them to sit.

"*Alright,*" he said, flipping open a notebook. "*Let's go one at a time. Mrs. Henshaw, since you were the one who witnessed the incident, let's start with you.*"

Valerie nodded, folding her hands neatly on the table. "*Of course.*"

The officer clicked his pen. "*Start from the beginning. What did you see?*"

Valerie took a breath, steady but measured. "*I was driving near the Willow Creek development last night. It was late—maybe a little after midnight. I had trouble sleeping, so I just went for a drive to clear my head.*"

The officer glanced up briefly. "*Alone?*"

"*Yes,*" Valerie said without hesitation. "*I do that sometimes.*"

He nodded, jotting something down. "*Go on.*"

"*I was passing the construction site when I saw a man near the back entrance of the office building. At first, I didn't think much of it—thought maybe he worked there. But then I saw him messing with the lock.*"

"*Messing with the lock how?*"

Valerie pressed her lips together, as if visualizing the moment. "*It looked like he was using some kind of tool to force it open. And after a few seconds, the door swung inward, and he went inside.*"

The officer tapped his pen against the pad. *"Did you see his face?"*

"No," Valerie said quickly. *"He had his back to me, and it was dark."*

"Height? Build? Clothing?"

She hesitated just long enough for the officer to glance up again. *"Maybe six feet? Medium build? He was wearing a dark hoodie."*

The officer wrote something down, then looked at her again. *"You said this was after midnight?"*

"Yes."

*"And you were **driving** by when you saw this?"*

"Yes," Valerie repeated, her voice steady.

The officer nodded, but there was a slight pause before he asked, *"How long were you stopped?"*

Celeste tensed slightly at the question. It seemed harmless, but something about the way he asked it made her uneasy.

"Not long," Valerie answered smoothly. *"A minute, maybe two."*

"You were parked?"

"*Yes.*"

"*Where?*"

Valerie hesitated. Just for a second. "*Across the street.*"

The officer's pen stilled briefly before he started writing again. "*Go on.*"

Valerie exhaled slowly. "*After he went inside, I didn't know what to do. I thought maybe I was overreacting, that maybe he **did** work there. But then he came back out a few minutes later—carrying something.*"

The officer's gaze sharpened slightly. "*Something?*"

"*Yes,*" Valerie said. "*It looked like he was hiding it under his jacket. I couldn't see exactly what it was, but it was small enough to conceal.*"

The officer leaned back slightly. "*And then?*"

"*He walked off,*" Valerie said. "*Disappeared down the street.*"

The officer was silent for a moment, tapping his pen against the table. Then he shifted his gaze to Celeste. "*Alright, Ms. Monroe. What did you see?*"

Celeste hesitated. "*I... I didn't see anything firsthand. Valerie told me about it this morning, and I encouraged her to come here.*"

31

The officer nodded slowly, then scribbled something in his notebook.

Celeste wasn't sure why, but the way he wrote things down made her stomach tighten.

"So," he said after a moment, *"you didn't witness anything yourself?"*

"No," she admitted. *"But I believe her. Valerie isn't the type to make something like this up."*

The officer looked at Valerie again, then back at Celeste. *"Alright,"* he said finally. *"We'll take down your statement and log the report. We may have some follow-up questions, depending on what the investigation turns up."*

Celeste exhaled, relieved that it was over. But something about the way the officer closed his notebook didn't sit right with her.

As they stood to leave, he glanced at Valerie one last time. *"You said you were parked across the street?"*

"Yes," Valerie said, forcing a small smile.

The officer nodded. *"That's interesting."*

Celeste felt a flicker of confusion. *"Why?"*

He shrugged. *"No cameras on that side."*

Valerie let out a soft laugh, shaking her head. *"Well, isn't that convenient?"*

The officer's smile appeared on his lips, yet it lacked the warmth that would light up his eyes. *"Yeah,"* he said, sliding his pen behind his ear. *"It is."*

———————

The officer's words lingered in Celeste's mind as she and Valerie left the station. The afternoon sun was beginning to dip below the horizon, casting long shadows on the pavement. Celeste tried to shake off the feeling of unease, attributing it to the stress of the day.

Once home, she went through the motions of her evening routine—feeding her cat, reheating leftovers, and settling onto the couch with a book. But the words on the page blurred together, her mind drifting back to the police station. The officer's expression, the way he had tapped his pen, and the peculiar emphasis on the lack of cameras all replayed in her thoughts.

She tried to dismiss it, telling herself that Valerie was her friend and had always been trustworthy. Yet, something in her gut wouldn't let it go. It was as if a small, persistent voice was whispering that there was more to the story than she had been told.

Celeste glanced at her phone, tempted to call Valerie and ask more questions, but she hesitated. Instead, she set the book aside and stared out the window, watching the neighborhood lights flicker to life. The police report was filed, and the day was done, but the feeling of something being amiss clung to her like a shadow.

As she finally drifted off to sleep, her dreams were filled with fragmented images—Valerie's forced smile, the officer's knowing look, and the empty street devoid of cameras.

———

Celeste pressed her key card against the scanner, the office door clicking open with a familiar beep. The morning hum of the building was already in full swing—colleagues chatting near the coffee station, the faint sound of keyboards clacking, the distant noise of a conference call bleeding through the glass-walled meeting rooms.

She made her way to her office, setting down her bag before pulling out her phone. A new text from Valerie.

> **Valerie:** *Any word from the police?*

Celeste checked her missed calls. Nothing. She started typing a response, but before she could send it, another message popped up.

> **Valerie:** *I just keep thinking... what if this guy tries something again? What if someone gets hurt because I spoke up too late?*

Celeste exhaled, rubbing her forehead. She hadn't thought about that. What if this wasn't just a one-time thing? What if they had reported it just in time?

Feeling a surge of conviction, she deleted her original message and typed a new one.

> **Celeste:** *Nothing yet, but I'm sure they're looking into it. You did the right thing, Val. We did the right thing.*

She hit send, then locked her phone and turned to her monitor. But before she could start her work, a voice from the doorway behind her cut through her thoughts.

"You hear about the break-in?"

Celeste glanced over her shoulder. Rachel, from IT, was leaning against the office door, sipping from a company-branded mug.

Celeste's pulse quickened. *"What break-in?"* she asked, feigning mild curiosity.

Rachel's eyes widened. *"Oh, it's all over the security channels. Someone hit the Willow Creek site a few nights ago. Nobody knows what was taken, but there's an internal inquiry happening. You'd think the company would've said something officially."*

Celeste felt a strange, twisting sensation in her stomach. The report she and Valerie had filed was already rippling through the company.

Rachel took another sip of coffee. *"I heard they're already looking at suspects."*

Celeste's breath hitched. *"Suspects?"*

Rachel nodded. *"Yeah, but it's all hush-hush. Probably why they haven't sent an official notice yet."* She leaned in closer with a secretive air. *"Between you and me, I bet they already know who it is. Probably some disgruntled employee."*

Celeste forced a small, nonchalant smile, but her hands were cold.

Rachel tilted her head. *"Why do you look so serious?"*

Celeste shook herself. *"No reason. Just... it's weird to hear about something like this happening so close to home."*

Rachel shrugged. *"Eh, it's corporate. Someone's always trying to get ahead, one way or another."*

The comment struck Celeste in a way she couldn't explain.

Before she could dwell on it, another text from Valerie buzzed in her hand.

> **Valerie:** *We should talk later. Maybe a phone call? Just in case this gets bigger than we expected.*

Celeste's stomach twisted tighter.

Just how big *was* this going to get?

———————

Celeste shut her laptop, leaning back in her chair as the last of her emails disappeared from view. The office was quieter now—most of her team had trickled out for lunch, leaving only the hum of overhead lights and the distant sound of a printer spitting out reports.

Her phone vibrated against her desk.

Valerie Henshaw Calling...

She exhaled before answering. *"Hey."*

"Hey," Valerie's voice was low, measured. *"You got a minute?"*

Celeste pushed away from her desk, glancing around. *"Yeah, what's up?"*

A pause. Then Valerie sighed. *"I just—I can't shake this feeling, Celeste. I keep thinking... what if this guy knows I saw him? What if he finds out I went to the police?"*

Celeste frowned. *"You didn't tell them your address, did you?"*

"Of course not," Valerie said quickly. *"But still... what if he works for the company? What if he knows who I am?"*

Celeste felt a prickle of unease. The thought hadn't occurred to her.

Valerie continued, her voice tightening. *"I keep replaying last night in my head. What if he saw* **me** *first? What if he wasn't just stealing something—what if he was casing the place? What if next time, it's not just a break-in?"*

Celeste sat up straighter. *"Val—"*

"I know, I know," Valerie rushed on. *"Maybe I'm overthinking. But Celeste, this could be* **big**. *This isn't some random petty theft. I keep thinking... what if it's bigger than we realize?"*

Celeste pressed her fingertips against her temple. *"What are you saying?"*

"I'm saying we need to make sure people **know** *what happened. If something happens later and we kept quiet —"* She stopped short, exhaling sharply. *"I don't want that on my conscience."*

Celeste hesitated. *"The police are already looking into it."*

"Are they?" Valerie countered. *"Or is this going to disappear like everything else does around here?"*

Celeste swallowed. Valerie wasn't wrong. They had watched HR sweep things under the rug before. Leadership never addressed real problems unless there was *pressure*.

"I don't know, Val..."

"Just... just be aware, okay?" Valerie softened her tone. *"You have more credibility in this company than I do. If people start asking about it, don't downplay it. Let them know it's serious."*

Celeste let out a slow breath. *"I don't want to spread rumors."*

"This isn't a rumor," Valerie said. *"It's the truth."*

Something about the way she said it made Celeste feel like a line had been drawn in the sand.

And she had already stepped over it.

———

CHAPTER THREE

A FRIEND'S WORD

*"He who does not bellow the truth when he knows the truth
makes himself the accomplice of liars and forgers."*
– Charles Péguy

Celeste sat at her desk, scanning through emails, when the office phone rang. She reached for it instinctively, barely looking up.

"Celeste Monroe," she answered.

"Celeste," Jason's voice came through, sharp with urgency. *"You hear about Damien?"*

Celeste sat up straighter, her heart skipping a beat. *"What do you mean?"*

Jason's voice dropped lower, a mix of curiosity and concern. *"I'll be over in a bit!"*

Call ends.

She balanced her coffee in one hand while scrolling through her inbox with the other, barely skimming the flood of unread messages. The office was unusually quiet that morning—no idle chatter, no lingering conversations near the coffee station. There was a heaviness in the air, something unspoken but palpable.

She glanced out toward Rachel's desk, expecting her usual morning greeting, but Rachel was locked in a hushed conversation with two other colleagues. Their voices were low, their expressions tight.

Celeste frowned. *Whaaat now?*

Before she could ask, Jason—a project manager from an adjacent team—showed up, tossing a file onto her desk. *"Wild morning, huh?"*

Celeste blinked. *"Is it?"*

Jason stopped, narrowing his eyes. *"You haven't heard?"*

Celeste set down her coffee. *"Heard what?"*

Jason whistled softly. *"They think Damien was the one who broke into Willow Creek."*

Celeste froze.

"Damien?" she repeated. *"As in Damien Carter?"*

Jason nodded. *"Yep. They're saying he was the one who broke into Willow Creek. Supposedly, security flagged something in the system. IT is involved now. Word is, he's being questioned. The whole thing's blowing up."*

Celeste's blood ran cold. Damien?

The quiet, unassuming guy from infrastructure? The one who never caused trouble and always kept to himself?

"No way," Celeste said, shaking her head, though her voice faltered. *"Damien? He has access, but I never thought—"*

"Yeah, well, you might want to think again."

Celeste felt her pulse tick up as a knot tightened in her stomach. The thought of Damien—an employee she'd worked with for years—being the one accused of breaking into the property was hard to reconcile. She had never known him to be anything but professional. He wasn't exactly social, but he was good at his job. Never would she think him to be the type to pull something like this.

Jason must have caught the doubt in her expression. *"Makes sense if you think about it. He had clearance to access the facility, right? Who else would know the ins and outs of the system?"*

Celeste didn't respond immediately. *Damien?* She hadn't considered who might be accused—she had only focused on the fact that someone *should* be.

Before she could process, her phone buzzed.

Valerie: *Call me when you get a chance.*

Celeste inhaled sharply, locking her screen.

She had a sinking feeling this was about to get a lot more complicated.

———

Celeste shut her office door before pressing the phone to her ear. *"Okay, I'm here. What's going on?"*

"Did you hear?" Valerie's voice was calm—too calm.

"About Damien? Yeah, Jason just told me."

Valerie sighed, as if the news was both expected and disappointing. *"I had a feeling they'd land on him."*

Celeste frowned. *"You...had a feeling?"*

"Well, yeah," Valerie said. *"It makes sense, doesn't it? He had access. He worked in infrastructure. He knew how to get in and out without tripping alarms."*

Celeste's stomach twisted. *"Yeah, but Val... what if it wasn't him?"*

A beat of silence. Then, Valerie let out a small, humorless laugh. *"Celeste."*

Celeste knew that tone. It was the same one Valerie used in meetings when someone suggested a completely unrealistic deadline or when an executive pretended a problem didn't exist. It was a *you're smarter than this* tone.

"*I'm just saying*," Celeste continued, trying to find the right words, "*we don't **know** it was him. We weren't there.*"

"*No, but I **was** there*," Valerie corrected. "*I know what I saw. And you know how this works—security isn't just pulling names out of a hat. If they're looking at Damien, there's a reason.*"

Celeste exhaled. *Right. There's a reason.*

"*You trust me, don't you?*" Valerie's voice softened.

Celeste closed her eyes for a second. "*Of course, I do.*"

"*Then don't overthink this*," Valerie said. "*We did the right thing. I know it's weird seeing someone you work with in this situation, but you can't let that shake you.*"

Celeste leaned against her desk, pressing her fingers to her temple. "*I just... I don't want to be part of ruining someone's life if they didn't actually do anything.*"

"*I get that*," Valerie said gently. "*But what about the alternative? What if we **hadn't** spoken up, and it **was** him? What if we had just ignored it and let something worse happen?*"

Celeste swallowed. She hadn't thought of it like that.

*"You and I—we did what we were **supposed** to do,"* Valerie continued. *"We saw something, we said something. If Damien is innocent, then that's for security and the police to figure out. But if he's guilty..."* She let the thought hang in the air.

Celeste sighed, her resistance crumbling. *"I guess you're right."*

"I know I am," Valerie said, her voice warm now, reassuring. *"Listen, I know this is weighing on you, but you don't have to carry this alone. I've got you, okay?"*

Celeste nodded absently, even though Valerie couldn't see her. *"Yeah. Okay."*

"Good," Valerie said. *"Now, I need you to do me a favor."*

Celeste straightened. *"What is it?"*

"People are going to start talking about this. If anyone asks you about what happened, just—don't minimize it. We need them to understand how serious this is."

Celeste hesitated. *"You mean, like... just confirm that there was a break-in?"*

*"Yes, but also that it **wasn't random**."* Valerie's voice was firm. *"This wasn't some kid looking for scrap metal. This was planned. You and I both know that."*

Celeste exhaled. *"Right."*

"Don't worry, just... be honest," Valerie said smoothly. *"That's what we've been doing from the start, right?"*

Celeste felt something flicker in the back of her mind, something she couldn't quite name. But she pushed it aside.

"Right," she repeated.

———

By mid-afternoon, the tension in the office had shifted from whispered speculation to outright conversation. The break-in wasn't just a passing rumor anymore—it was *the topic.* People who never cared about company security were suddenly acting like investigators, swapping theories over coffee and scrolling through internal emails for any hint of official confirmation.

Celeste tried to focus on her work, but her eyes kept darting toward her inbox. No updates from the police. No messages from HR. Just a lingering, unsettled feeling in her chest.

Her office door was half closed, half open, and she sat at her desk, typing and stopping—in an ongoing rotation. She had just spent the last two hours composing an update on the logistics report for the senior management team, a task that felt like it would never end. Her eyes kept flicking back to her phone, wondering if she'd get another call from Valerie—maybe about that police update, maybe just to check in.

Jason appeared at her door, leaning against the frame. *"So,"* he said, lowering his voice, *"what do you think?"*

Celeste blinked. *"About what?"*

Pushing the door fully open, Jason gave her a pointed look. *"Come on. The Damien thing."*

Celeste sighed, keeping her voice even. *"I don't know. It's not really our place to speculate."*

"Maybe not," Jason admitted. *"But I do know that security flagged something in the logs. So either Damien was doing something shady, or someone really wanted to make it look like he was."*

Celeste's stomach flipped. She hadn't considered that angle.

Jason watched her, waiting for a response. She hesitated, then exhaled. *"Look, all I know is that this wasn't random. Whoever did it, it was planned."*

Jason raised an eyebrow. *"Planned?"*

Celeste nodded. *"Yeah. It wasn't just someone looking for scrap metal or a crime of opportunity. They knew what they were doing."*

Jason tilted his head slightly. *"And you know this how?"*

She hesitated. *"I just... I have reason to believe."*

Jason studied her for a moment, then smirked. *"You know something."*

Celeste shook her head quickly. *"No, it's not like that—"*

Jason let out a low laugh, almost like he was trying to reassure her, but there was something calculated in his tone. *"I get it, Celeste. It's weird. But I guess we have to trust the process. I mean, if they're looking at Damien, there's probably a good reason, right?"*

Celeste rubbed her forehead. *"Yeah, that's what everyone's saying. But, honestly, sometimes I think we're all just jumping to conclusions. I mean, we weren't even there. How do we know for sure?"*

"True, but I think you should be careful what you say about all of this, Celeste," Jason said, his voice shifting slightly. *"You know HR's been breathing down everyone's neck about the whole thing."*

Celeste frowned. *"I wasn't planning on talking about it outside the team."*

"I'm just saying," Jason continued, *"it's a touchy subject. And if this goes any further—well, you've gotta make sure you're not, you know, getting caught in a web yourself."*

Celeste blinked. *"Caught in a web?"*

"I just mean, don't get too casual with who you talk to. Sometimes people take things the wrong way." Jason's voice turned almost friendly again. *"I don't want to see anything happen to you. You've got a lot riding on this, Celeste."*

She frowned again, unsettled. *"Right, I know. Thanks, Jason."*

"Relax," Jason said, raising a hand in surrender. *"I'm just saying, if you've got insight, maybe you should be careful about who you share it with. People are watching this situation closely."*

With that, Jason walked off, leaving Celeste staring at the space where he used to be, suddenly feeling much less sure of herself.

She drooped forward in her chair, her mind racing. *Was she being too open?* Jason's words echoed in her mind. Had she said too much?

Just as she was about to go over it again, her phone buzzed again—it was Valerie.

"Hey, Val," Celeste said, trying to keep her voice steady.

"Hey, sweetie! How's your day going?" Valerie's voice was light, almost cheerful.

"I'm fine, just working through some things. How about you?" Celeste kept the conversation neutral, not wanting to get into her conversation with Jason.

"Same here. Actually, I wanted to ask you about a quick thing. Did you—um—did you mention anything to Jason or anyone else about Damien?" Valerie's voice had suddenly dropped a few octaves.

Celeste hesitated. *"Well... yeah. He asked me about the whole situation, and I just—y'know—was talking. I didn't think it was that big of a deal."*

There was a brief silence on the other end, followed by a soft, almost imperceptible sigh from Valerie. *"You have to be careful about who you talk to about this stuff, Celeste. It's one thing to talk to me, but when you start telling people who don't have the full picture..."*

"I just said what happened," Celeste said quickly. *"I didn't say anything out of line."*

"I know, I know," Valerie replied, trying to soothe her. *"But it's important to keep things tight. The last thing we need is for someone to start questioning your involvement. The less people know, the better, right?"*

Celeste's stomach churned a little, but she couldn't pinpoint why. *"Right, of course."*

"Good," Valerie said softly. *"I'm just looking out for you. It's not just about us now. We need to be smart. Everyone's watching, and we can't risk looking guilty just because of something we said."*

Celeste swallowed. *"Yeah. I hear you. I'll be more careful."*

"Great. Let's keep it tight, okay?"

"Okay," Celeste agreed, her voice betraying her uncertainty.

As she ended the call, Celeste leaned back in her chair, her fingers pressed to her lips. *Be careful. Everyone's watching.*

---

1 WEEK AFTER THE BREAK-IN

Celeste was halfway through her workload and her second cup of afternoon coffee when her inbox pinged with a new email marked **"URGENT"**.

Subject: HR Compliance Inquiry – Private & Confidential

Her stomach dropped.

She clicked it open.

> *"Celeste,*
>
> *We'd like to schedule a brief discussion regarding the recent security report. Please let us know your availability this week."*

- *HR Compliance Team*

Celeste's grip on her mug   tightened. **HR Compliance Team.** Not just HR—*compliance.* That was never good.

HR? Compliance? Why are they pulling me in?

Her hands hovered over her keyboard. Valerie hadn't mentioned anything about HR involvement. She had made it sound like the police would handle it, and that would be that. Celeste prided herself on her unwavering integrity, always choosing to do the right thing, even when it was difficult. It was a trait that had earned her both respect and, occasionally, unwanted attention.

Her mind immediately jumped back to her conversation with Jason. *Had someone reported her for talking about the situation?* She had always been a staunch advocate for transparency and accountability, values that sometimes put her at odds with others who preferred to keep things under wraps.

A quiet panic settled in her bones. She knew she had done nothing wrong, but the uncertainty gnawed at her. The thought of being scrutinized for her actions, actions she believed were right, was unsettling.

Before she could spiral, her phone vibrated.

Valerie Henshaw Calling...

Celeste stared at the screen for a second. She hesitated an additional tick, then answered. *"Tell me you just got the same email I did."*

There was a pause. Then, Valerie's voice, smooth as ever. *"What email?"*

"HR just emailed me. They want to talk about the break-in."

Another pause. Then—*"Oh. Well... that's normal, right? They probably just want to document everything."*

Celeste frowned. *"You're the one who filed the report. Why aren't they calling you in first?"*

Valerie let out a light laugh. *"Sweetie, you were there when I reported it. They probably just want to verify what we told them."*

Celeste exhaled. *"Are they calling you in, too?"*

A pause.

Then—*"Not yet, but I'm sure they will."*

Something about that answer made Celeste pause.

Not yet?

That didn't make sense. She was the one who filed the damn report. If HR was looking into this, shouldn't they be talking to Valerie first?

"Celeste," Valerie's voice pulled her back, light and reassuring. *"This is just HR doing their due diligence. It's nothing."*

Celeste ran a hand through her hair. *"I don't know. It feels... big."*

Valerie laughed softly. *"Sweetie, you think everything feels big. It's your greatest strength and your biggest flaw."*

Celeste's lips parted slightly, but she didn't know how to respond.

"Look," Valerie continued, her tone easy, practiced. *"They'll probably just ask what you know, what you told the police, and remind you to be careful about workplace gossip. No big deal."*

"Right…"

"And remember, we haven't done anything wrong," Valerie added, her voice dipping lower, more serious. *"We saw something. We reported it. If people want to question that, that's on them. Not us."*

Celeste nodded absently, but her thoughts kept circling back.

Why wasn't HR questioning Valerie first?

Why did it suddenly feel like Celeste was at the center of this, when Valerie was the one who started it?

And why—*why*—did Valerie's reassurances leave her feeling unsettled?

———————

Celeste smoothed her blazer as she stepped into the HR office, where a woman in a charcoal suit waited with a legal pad in front of her.

"*Ms. Monroe*," she said with a professional smile. "*Please, have a seat.*"

Celeste sat, forcing herself to remain calm.

"*I appreciate you taking the time to speak with us,*" the woman continued, flipping open the legal pad. "*This is just a routine discussion to ensure we have a full understanding of recent events.*"

Celeste nodded. "*Of course.*"

"*To start—how did you become involved in this report?*"

Celeste folded her hands in her lap. "*Valerie Henshaw told me she witnessed the break-in, and I encouraged her to report it.*"

"*Encouraged?*"

Celeste hesitated. "*Well, she was unsure at first, but I told her it was the right thing to do.*"

The woman scribbled something down.

"*And at any point, did you personally witness any suspicious activity?*"

"*No,*" Celeste said quickly. "*I only know what Valerie told me.*"

Another scribble. "*And in your discussions with other employees, how have you spoken about the incident?*"

Celeste frowned. "*I... haven't gone into detail. People have been talking about it, but I haven't said anything that wasn't already public knowledge.*"

"*Public knowledge?*" The woman raised an eyebrow.

Celeste swallowed.

Had she said too much?

"*Ms. Monroe,*" the woman continued, flipping to another page, "*we want to remind you that any statements you make regarding an open investigation—whether to employees, leadership, or external parties—could have unintended legal consequences.*"

Celeste felt her blood run cold.

Legal consequences?

"*We understand that workplace discussions happen, but we strongly advise against engaging in any further speculation. This is a sensitive matter.*"

Celeste nodded slowly. "*I understand.*"

The woman closed her legal pad. "*That's all we need for now. Thank you for your time.*"

Celeste barely muttered a goodbye as she stood and left the office.

Her stomach felt hollow.

Legal consequences.

This was no longer just office gossip.

It was bigger than she'd ever expected.

Celeste stepped out of the HR office, her heels clicking sharply against the polished floor. She felt lightheaded, her mind still reeling from the word that had lodged itself deep in her chest.

Legal consequences.

Her phone buzzed. Valerie.

Celeste answered immediately. *"Val—"*

"Sweetie, breathe." Valerie's voice was smooth, calm. *"You sound like you just ran a marathon."*

Celeste pushed open the stairwell door, needing a quiet place to think. *"I just walked out of HR. They warned me about—about legal repercussions."*

"Oh, please." Valerie let out a soft chuckle. *"That's just corporate covering their ass."*

Celeste gripped the railing, her pulse hammering. *"It didn't feel like that, Val. They were serious. They asked me about what*

I've said to other employees. It sounded like—like I could be held liable."

"Celeste." Valerie's tone was gentle, almost patronizing. *"We haven't done anything wrong. You told the truth. I told the truth. The only people who need to worry are the guilty ones."*

Celeste exhaled slowly. *"Right... right."*

Valerie continued, her voice warm. *"Look, this will blow over. You'll see. We did the right thing."*

Celeste nodded, even though Valerie couldn't see her. *"Yeah. I guess so."*

"Good girl." Valerie's voice softened. *"Now, let's get back to work, okay?"*

***

2 WEEKS AFTER THE BREAK-IN

Celeste was finishing a spreadsheet analysis when an email notification popped up.

Subject: Legal Notice – Carter v. APEX Logistics

Her heart raced.

With shaky hands, she clicked it open.

To: All Parties Concerned

"This serves as formal notification that Mr. Damien Carter, via legal representation, is initiating action against APEX Logistics and associated individuals for defamation, wrongful accusation, and damages related to professional and personal harm.

Legal counsel will be in contact to discuss the next steps."

- *Carter & Associates, LLP*

Celeste's vision blurred. Her name wasn't listed—but "*associated individuals*" could only mean one thing.

Her phone buzzed again. Another call from Valerie.

She answered without hesitation. "*Did you see the email?*"

"*I did,*" Valerie said, but she didn't sound worried. "*I expected something like this.*"

Celeste let out a breath. "*Val, this is real. Damien's suing.*"

"No, sweetie, Damien's bluffing." Valerie's tone remained effortlessly calm. *"That's what people do when they're guilty. They try to scare you into silence."*

Celeste closed her eyes. *"What if he's not guilty?"*

Silence.

Then, Valerie sighed. *"Celeste, you need to trust me. I saw what I saw. Don't let a scared man with a lawyer make you second-guess yourself."*

Celeste pressed a hand to her temple. *"But if this goes to court—"*

"Then the truth wins."

Celeste exhaled. *"I hope you're right."*

Valerie's voice was gentle but firm. *"I am."*

But for the first time, Celeste wasn't entirely sure.

———————

Celeste sat at her desk, staring at the email.

She could still hear Valerie's voice in her head.

"Sweetie, breathe." *"This will blow over."* *"He's just bluffing."*

But now, staring at those cold, formal words from **Carter & Associates, LLP**, she wasn't sure if she believed that anymore.

A lawsuit.

Her heart pounded as she imagined herself sitting in a courtroom, answering questions, watching lawyers twist her words.

"What if he's not guilty?"

She had said it out loud this time. And Valerie had *hesitated* before shutting her down.

That hesitation clung to Celeste like a weight she couldn't shake.

———

CHAPTER FOUR

NO TURNING BACK

"We are never so defenseless against suffering as when we love."
– Sigmund Freud

1 *MONTH AFTER THE BREAK-IN*

Just as she was logging off for the day, a new email popped up.

Subject: URGENT – Legal Counsel Meeting Invitation

Her pulse quickened.

She opened it.

Mandatory Legal Briefing — 10:00 AM, Conference Room C
Carter v. APEX Logistics | Direct Involvement Notification: CELESTE MONROE

To: Celeste Monroe

"Due to recent developments, you are required to attend a legal briefing regarding pending litigation involving Damien Carter. Please report to the legal department at 10 AM tomorrow."

- *APEX Logistics Legal Division*

Celeste's breath hitched.

This wasn't just a corporate issue anymore. This was personal.

She wasn't just involved in a lawsuit.

She was being *named* in it.

Celeste sat on her couch, her laptop open, fingers hovering over the keyboard. She had spent the last hour researching defamation lawsuits, trying to understand what she was up against.

And what she found?

It was terrifying.

Defamation cases could take months, sometimes years. Legal fees alone could drain savings before a trial even started.

She checked her bank account balance.

She was financially stable—but a long lawsuit could change that.

Her stomach churned.

She grabbed her phone and dialed Valerie.

"*Hey, sweetie,*" Valerie answered smoothly.

"*I'm named in the lawsuit.*" Celeste's voice was tight.

A pause. Then—"*What?*" Valerie's tone sharpened, just for a second. "*Are you sure?*"

Celeste clenched her jaw. "*I got the email a little while ago. Legal wants to meet with me tomorrow.*"

Another pause. Then Valerie sighed. "*Celeste, listen to me. The company will handle this. You are not responsible for any of this.*"

"*But my name is in it, Val.*"

"*That doesn't mean anything,*" Valerie countered quickly. "*Damien's lawyers are probably naming everyone connected to the report just to apply pressure. They do that all the time.*"

Celeste gripped the phone tighter. "*And what if they don't drop it?*"

Valerie exhaled. *"Then they'll settle. Corporate lawsuits rarely go to trial. Trust me, you have nothing to worry about."*

Celeste bit her lip. She wanted to believe Valerie. She wanted to believe that this would go away.

But something in her gut told her this wasn't going to be that simple.

Celeste hadn't slept more than two hours.

She had spent the night tossing beneath tangled sheets, every attempt at rest disturbed by circling thoughts. The email had arrived just before 5 p.m. the night before—short, sterile, and impossible to forget.

Mandatory Legal Briefing — 10:00 AM, Conference Room C
Carter v. APEX Logistics | Direct Involvement Notification: CELESTE MONROE

She'd read it three times in a row, assuming there had been some mistake. Then five more times in growing silence. The words didn't change. *"Direct involvement."* Her name. *Specifically.*

That phrase had taken up residence in her mind overnight, growing heavier with each passing hour. By sunrise, she felt like she'd been standing in a courtroom already, judged and found wanting—without understanding why.

The morning passed in a blur. She skipped coffee. Couldn't stomach breakfast. Showered too long but still felt unclean, like shame clung to her skin. She double-checked the email, then her calendar, then the email again.

By the time she arrived at the office, she was in a quiet fog.

She kept her head down on the walk to Conference Room C, unsure who might already know. The hallway felt louder than usual. Every laugh or passing glance registered as a threat. Her coworkers' casual greetings felt foreign, like distant echoes from a life she no longer lived.

Inside the conference room, the mood was more subdued— legal counsel from Compliance, a senior HR representative, and two others she didn't recognize. A thick manila envelope sat at each chair. She recognized her own name again on the label, printed in all caps: **MONROE, CELESTE.**

She slid into the seat quietly, smoothing the fabric of her blouse as if presentation still mattered. Her heart was pounding.

The lead legal counsel—a tall, calm man with a stiff collar and unreadable face—began speaking, but she couldn't focus. The fluorescent lights buzzed above her, too loud. The words came and went: *...disclosure... standard notification... named parties... cooperating witness... legal representation advised...*

Celeste stared down at the envelope. Her name was beginning to look unfamiliar. Foreign.

How did it get here?

All she had ever tried to do was help. To support a friend. To stand by someone she trusted—someone who *needed* her.

And now she was being blamed.

Had her kind heart led her into a trap?

The thought made her stomach twist. It didn't feel fair. It didn't feel *true.* But fairness and truth didn't seem to have much say in legal matters.

Celeste exhaled slowly, blinking hard. *Stay grounded.* She reminded herself of the values that had shaped her decisions— loyalty, integrity, faith. She *believed* she had done the right thing. Even now, when the path ahead felt like it was crumbling beneath her, she needed that belief to anchor her.

One hand moved to the envelope.

She peeled it open, careful not to tear it, and unfolded the letter inside.

RE: Carter v. APEX Logistics et al.

"You are hereby notified that you have been named in connection with the pending legal matter concerning Damien Carter.

*As a contributing party and material witness, you
are required to..."*

She stopped reading.

There it was again. *Contributing party.* Like an accusation
wrapped in formality.

Her pulse thudded in her ears. The conference room faded. She
didn't hear the rest of the legal briefing. She didn't feel the
chair under her or the pen she clutched in her hand.

She only felt the weight of the truth crashing down:

This wasn't theoretical anymore.

She was in it now.

And there *was no turning back.*

Valerie had barely slept.

It wasn't anxiety that kept her up, not really—it was more
like... strategy.

She had laid in bed wide awake, staring at the ceiling fan as it
made slow, lazy rotations overhead. Nathan had fallen asleep
sometime after midnight, but Valerie's thoughts remained

tangled, darting between what Celeste had told her on the phone and what the email from APEX Legal had confirmed.

Celeste was being named.

Officially.

Valerie rolled over on the sofa now, dressed in a oversized robe and leggings, nursing her second cup of coffee while watching Nathan move through the kitchen.

"You want me to heat up something before I head out?" he asked, already halfway into his sports jacket.

"No, I'm fine," she said quickly. *"I probably couldn't eat if I tried."*

Nathan paused, picking up on the edge in her voice. *"Still thinking about the lawsuit stuff?"*

Valerie exhaled slowly, swirling the last bit of coffee in her mug. *"Yeah... Celeste called me last night. She's spiraling."*

"Spiraling how?"

"She got the email—she's being named directly now. She sounded like she was five minutes from a breakdown." Valerie's tone was flat, like she was reciting weather.

Nathan tilted his head. *"That's... serious, right?"*

Valerie shrugged, lips pursed. "*I mean, yeah. Someone's going to have to take the fall for the Carter mess. And between you and me...*" She lowered her voice just enough. "*Ms. Perfect has finally found herself in a pickle.*"

Nathan raised a brow. "*You don't sound too torn up about it.*"

Valerie smiled, but it didn't quite reach her eyes. "*I tried to help. I **did** help. Everything I gave her—the info, the support, the late nights running scenarios... I didn't have to do any of that. But now it's like I'm being dragged into something I didn't ask for.*"

"*You **are** being dragged in, right?*" Nathan asked, suddenly more alert. "*They named you too?*"

Valerie looked out the window. "*No. Not officially. Not yet.*" She didn't add the rest: that the phrasing in her own legal email had been vague—"*may be contacted further.*" That the envelope she'd received didn't say much, only that she should prepare to clarify statements she'd made four weeks prior.

But she wasn't about to worry out loud. She had to look calm, helpful, innocent.

"*It's just a lot,*" she said instead. "*I'm doing everything I can to stay above water.*"

Nathan leaned down and kissed her forehead. "*You always do.*"

She smiled at that—soft and gracious—and waited until the door shut behind him before letting it drop.

The smile, the mask.

She walked into the dining room and sat down, glancing at her phone. No new messages. She knew exactly where Celeste was: in the 10 Legal meeting. Probably panicking. Probably wondering what she should do next.

The phone buzzed in her hand.

CELESTE MONROE CALLING...

Valerie stared at it. Let it ring. She counted the seconds: 1... 2... 3...

She knew the decent thing would be to answer. To reassure her. To act like the concerned friend.

But she didn't.

Instead, she watched the screen go dark.

She set the phone down—face down—and picked up her envelope again, unopened.

A whisper of a smile returned.

Let Celeste unravel a little. It might even be good for her.

———

The phone had long since gone dark.

Valerie leaned back in her chair, envelope untouched on the table beside her.

Outside the window, the sun had risen just a little too confidently—like it didn't know, or didn't care, that the world was a mess.

She sighed and stared at nothing for a moment, her hand idly tracing the edge of the coffee mug. She hadn't always felt this bitter. That had crept in slowly. Like mold.

It had started with Celeste.

Celeste Monroe—who didn't even try that hard and still got the recognition. Celeste, who breezed through presentations with that effortless poise. Celeste, who said all the right things, wore all the right outfits, and somehow made upper management hang on her every word.

Valerie remembered the day they met.

A training event. Logistics team.

She'd noticed Celeste immediately: poised, professional, and just a little bit too polished. The kind of woman who made other women feel tired.

But Celeste had been friendly. Open. Vulnerable, even. That whole thing about her mom in hospice? That had made Valerie drop her guard. She'd felt needed, seen. Important.

That's how it always starts, isn't it? One moment you're comforting someone, the next you're measuring yourself against them. Wondering why you're not the one being applauded in the boardroom.

Valerie was older, wiser, and—if she was being honest—far more strategic. But the world didn't reward loyalty or longevity. It rewarded sparkle. And Celeste sparkled.

And then came the promotion.

The one Valerie got.

The one Celeste didn't.

Valerie still smiled about that, sometimes. She'd worked the right channels, played the right people. Celeste had been blindsided. She'd said all the right congratulatory words, but her eyes told the truth. She was devastated.

And that should've been enough.

But it wasn't.

Because with that promotion came access.

Contracts. Data. Decision-making authority.

And one particular opportunity: a quiet, high-value award in the works for a legacy partner. Tens of millions of dollars on the line.

Valerie had a *friend* who ran a shell firm—on paper, clean and certified. Behind the scenes, a useful funnel. If she could steer the award that way, skim just enough for a *"consulting fee,"* then she and Nathan could finally stop worrying about their anemic retirement account.

God knew they needed it.

Valerie had always been bad with money. Shoes, getaways, her daughter's *custom-themed birthday parties*. No one told her that forty-five would arrive so quickly or so empty-handed. The idea of being broke *and* invisible terrified her.

She deserved comfort. And this contract was going to be her ticket.

Until Celeste started poking around. Asking too many questions. Running internal compliance reports and *flagging things she didn't even understand*. Celeste was always like that—eager to help, always digging in where she didn't belong.

She was going to ruin everything. Not on purpose. But the result would be the same.

Valerie could feel the panic rising even now, just remembering it. The way the walls started closing in. The timeline shrinking. The file she needed—secured and locked in the shared database—suddenly became restricted after Celeste made a report.

And so, Valerie did what she had to do.

She removed the guardrails.

After-hours access.

Admin override credentials.

One swipe, one copy, one encrypted flash drive.

She told herself it was temporary.

Just until she could *fix* the system.

Just until the award went through.

But deep down, she knew. That moment—the stealing of the file—was the point of no return.

———

The hallway felt like a pressure chamber.

Celeste stepped out of the conference room and pressed her back against the cool wall. Her hands were trembling, and she realized she had balled them into fists so tight her fingernails had left tiny crescents in her palm.

The letter from the general counsel was now folded sharply in her bag, but its weight felt like a brick.

Her name.

On official letterhead.

Involved in software theft.

Celeste blinked hard, trying to keep the tears at bay. She needed answers. Clarity. Sanity.

She fumbled for her phone and hit the contact without thinking. *Valerie Henshaw*. Her lifeline. The only one who knew the full scope of what had been happening these past few weeks. The only one who might understand the terror clawing at her throat.

It rang.

And rang.

And rang.

No answer.

Straight to voicemail.

Celeste stared down at the phone in disbelief, as if it might change its mind and start ringing again.

"*Valerie...*" she whispered, nearly a plea.

She pressed the phone to her ear, recording a message through the growing lump in her throat.

"*Hey... I, um... I just left the meeting. It's bad, Val. Like... worse than I imagined. I'm being named. I don't even—*"

Her voice cracked. *"I don't know what's happening, but I'm scared. Please. Call me when you can. I need you."*

She ended the call and stared at the wall. Everything felt tilted—like the building was sliding sideways beneath her.

What had she missed?

How had this escalated so quickly?

Celeste had done everything by the book. Every process followed, every oversight reported. So why did it feel like she was the one who had done something wrong?

Her phone stayed quiet.

She didn't know that miles away, Valerie was staring at the same screen...

Watching her name flash across it...

And choosing silence.

Valerie's finger hovered over the screen as the call came in.

Celeste's name—glowing, hopeful.

She felt nothing.

Well—no, that wasn't true.

She felt power.

And power, finally, felt good.

She let the phone ring until it stopped.

———

CHAPTER FIVE

THE LONG GAME

"Some people are not loyal to you. They are loyal to their need of you. Once their needs change, so does their loyalty."
— *Unknown*

18 *MONTHS PRIOR TO THE BREAK-IN*

Valerie had parked at the far end of the lot that day, away from the prying eyes of coworkers and the buzz of the main entrance. She sat in her car, watching Celeste stride confidently into APEX HQ, heels clicking, dress tailored, energy magnetic.

"Of course they picked her," Valerie muttered, pulling at the peeling leather on her steering wheel. *"Ms. Perfect."*

The announcement came just two hours earlier: Celeste would lead the Johnson & Harlan pitch — a $4.3 million opportunity. Valerie had wanted it. Had hinted at it. Had practically built the client relationship herself.

But she didn't look the part. Didn't sound the part. And Celeste? She floated in like she belonged in front of every client table.

It wasn't the first time. It wouldn't be the last.

That night, Valerie pulled out a spiral notebook and began listing names. Projects. Outcomes. Places she could adjust things — just slightly — without setting off alarms. She told herself it wasn't sabotage. It was survival.

A month later, Valerie wiped the fog from the inside of the windshield with the sleeve of her blazer. The APEX Logistics building loomed ahead, bathed in the artificial glow of the parking lot lights. She hadn't even turned off the engine. Her fingers gripped the steering wheel like she was holding onto something that might slip away.

She stared at the glass doors, at the reflection of herself looking back — tired, aging, and invisible.

Inside, Celeste was probably already rehearsing her part for the upcoming client presentation. Valerie knew the drill: catering orders, slide decks, client bios, coordinated outfits. The entire project team would orbit around Celeste today like she was the sun. And Valerie? A starless, cold rock, floating somewhere in the periphery.

"She's good," Valerie mumbled. *"Too good."*

Nathan had said it just last week. *"You should be learning from that girl"*, he'd told her, flipping through their household budget. *"She's the kind of woman who retires early. Look at you… still playing catch-up with our credit cards."*

The humiliation still sat heavy in her chest. That, and the $21,700 balance on their main Visa. The spoiled child. The overpriced braces. The lake house rental they couldn't really afford but booked anyway because Madison *deserved nice things.*

Valerie's lips pressed into a thin line. Celeste hadn't even wanted the spotlight, but somehow always ended up in it. Her name was on all the right projects, all the right performance reviews, all the right people's lips. And yet, Valerie — *the one who stayed late, who trained others, who bled for the department* — was constantly passed over.

But not anymore.

She reached for her phone, pulling up the calendar. The client presentation was scheduled for Friday. Valerie had been copied on the invite — as a courtesy. Celeste had sent a cheerful follow-up that morning: *"Val, I'd love your thoughts before the run-through!"*

Valerie didn't respond.

Instead, she opened a blank draft email and started typing a message to one of the vendor partners. Nothing major. Just a few suggestions about alternate figures for last quarter's fulfillment metrics — numbers she knew Celeste hadn't cross-verified yet. Then she set a calendar invite for Celeste's one-on-one with leadership... for the wrong time. Just ten minutes off. Barely enough to cause suspicion.

But enough to rattle.

She sat back, reread the email, then deleted it. Not yet.

This would take time. Planning. Precision. She needed to look like a bystander, not the hand that set the fire.

Valerie finally turned off the engine and gathered her bag. Before stepping out into the morning air, she whispered a scripture under her breath.

"Be wise as serpents, and harmless as doves."

Then she smiled.

———

Valerie stepped into the lobby just as Marcus from Finance was swiping his badge at the elevators.

"Morning," he said casually, giving her a polite nod.

She returned it with a sunny smile that didn't quite... *"Good morning, Marcus! Big week ahead, huh?"*

He nodded again, but his expression didn't change. The elevator doors opened. Valerie stepped in beside him, aware that he didn't press the button for his floor. He waited until it was just the two of them to speak.

"Hey, not sure if you saw, but Celeste and her team will be using the third-floor conference space today. They asked for privacy ahead of the client walkthrough," he said pointedly.

Valerie blinked. *"Oh, did they? That's... good to know."*

Marcus gave her a look — not mean, just weary. He didn't trust her. He didn't need to say it.

The elevator stopped on three. Valerie smiled sweetly, said nothing, and let the doors close again as she ascended to the executive floor.

She hated that people saw through her. Hated that she couldn't quite cover up her own ambition with enough Bible verses or workplace platitudes to seem harmless. They liked Celeste better — of course they did. Celeste didn't *try* to impress anyone. She simply did. Her results spoke volumes. Her demeanor soothed. She remembered people's kids' names, brought snacks to team meetings, showed up on time and stayed late when needed — without the performative sighing that Valerie had perfected.

Even worse, Celeste made it look *easy*. And she was *nice*. Not fake-nice. Not I'm-pretending-to-care-for-the-sake-of-politics nice. Actual, honest-to-God kindness.

It made Valerie sick.

Upstairs, she breezed past the receptionist with a warm, *"Hey, girl!"* before settling into her office. She made a show of pulling out her planner, flipping to a page titled *"Goals & Gratitude,"* and writing:

I am a servant leader. I uplift those around me. Today, I choose integrity.

She paused, stared at the words, then smirked. What a load of crap.

Her phone lit up with a text — a photo from a colleague in the breakroom.

> **PHOTO:** *Celeste standing near the whiteboard, laughing, holding a dry-erase marker. Behind her, a bulleted agenda with her name circled in red at the top.*

> **TEXT:** Looks like your protégé's taking the reins

Valerie stared at the image for a moment too long. Then typed back:

> **REPLY:** I'm so proud of her! She deserves this.

A lie.

What she really wanted to write was: *She doesn't know what she's walking into.* But that would seem... jealous. Petty. And Valerie had mastered the art of appearing above reproach.

People might not like her — but they couldn't pin anything *real* on her. Not yet.

The truth was, she'd been playing the long game for a while now. Planting seeds. Whispering suggestions. Nudging key people toward new opinions. *"Be careful with Celeste,"* she'd said in confidence once to a VP, *"She tends to get overwhelmed under pressure. Just something I've noticed — not gossip, just concerned."*

She'd smiled when she said it. Even put her hand over her heart like it hurt her to say so.

But it worked.

She remembered the look on Celeste's face last quarter when she was unexpectedly passed over for a leadership roundtable she'd clearly been groomed for. The disappointment. The confusion.

Valerie had been *so supportive* — took her out for lunch, bought her soup, patted her hand and said, *"Don't worry, sweetie. God's timing, not ours."*

It had taken everything in her not to laugh into her Caesar salad.

Still, it hadn't been enough. Celeste continued to rise, somehow. One failed opportunity wouldn't keep her down for long—she was too good. Which meant Valerie had to be better. Or at least more strategic.

That's when the idea first formed. Not the whole plan—just a seed. If Celeste kept outshining her, the only way to fix the imbalance was to *tilt the scale.*

She opened her email and started composing a draft to her old friend Craig—the one she used to work with at Monarch Systems, now head of procurement for a mid-sized government contractor. The same friend who was eyeing a multimillion-dollar logistics support contract coming up for renewal. The same contract Valerie *just happened* to have backend access to.

> *"Hey Craig! Hope you and Marie are doing great. Quick question — would love to get your eyes on something. Think it could be a win-win for both of us..."*

She stared at the blinking cursor, then minimized the window. Not yet. Not today. She needed to keep playing the role.

Across the building, Celeste was leading a room full of stakeholders through a pitch that would likely land her more praise, more visibility, and maybe even a fast track to executive leadership.

Valerie was quietly rearranging the dominos.

12 MONTHS PRIOR TO THE BREAK-IN

The hum of espresso machines and quiet indie music filled the air inside Milo's Café, a cozy spot tucked between a dog boutique and a flower shop downtown. Jason sat at the window seat, scrolling through emails on his phone until he spotted her.

"*Hey*," Celeste greeted as she walked in, her black trench coat still dusted with the morning chill. "*Sorry I'm late.*"

Jason stood and gave her a quick hug. "*You're fine. I grabbed your usual.*"

She smiled, touched. "*You remembered.*"

"*Of course. Chai latte, extra hot, almond milk, and just a whisper of honey. You're very predictable.*"

They sat down across from each other. It had been a while — too long, really. Life had gotten busy, and work always seemed to find a way of crawling into their weekends.

"*So?*" Jason asked, stirring his coffee. "*What's going on? You sounded... tight on the phone.*"

Celeste exhaled, rubbing her temples. "*It's just been a long week. Valerie keeps pushing these deadlines up and then making 'adjustments' after we've already submitted draft materials. It's like I'm walking on eggshells trying not to make her look bad.*"

Jason leaned back, his expression unreadable.

Celeste took a sip of her drink and sighed. "*But then she turns around and says the kindest things to me — like how much she believes in my leadership potential and how I'm the only one she trusts to handle sensitive client comms. It's just... I don't know. Confusing sometimes."*

Jason tilted his head. *"Celeste... has it ever occurred to you that maybe she's doing both things **on purpose**?"*

She frowned. *"What do you mean?"*

He hesitated, choosing his words carefully. *"Let's just say... I've heard a few things. From someone who used to work in her department."*

Celeste stiffened a little. *"Like what?"*

Jason stirred his drink again, eyes fixed on the swirling foam. *"There's this saying — you've probably heard it. 'The most dangerous snake is the one that smiles the widest.'"*

Celeste gave a weak chuckle. *"That's dramatic."*

He smiled, but there was no warmth in it. *"Yeah. So is the Bible verse on her desk. Doesn't make it any less true."*

"Jason..."

"I'm not saying she's out to get you," he said quickly. *"But I've seen this before. People who play both sides of the fence. Who lift you up just high enough to pull the rug out when you least expect it. All I'm saying is... be careful. Don't give away too much. Keep a little something for yourself."*

Celeste looked down at her hands, suddenly unsure what to say. Valerie had *always* been there for her — in her corner, praying with her after her mom passed, talking her down from so many career cliffs.

"She's never done anything to make me doubt her," she murmured.

Jason nodded slowly. *"Not yet."*

There was a long pause. Then he leaned forward.

"I care about you, Cel. And I know how much you want to see the good in people. Just promise me something?"

"What?"

"If the time comes — and you feel something's off — don't talk yourself out of it just because you love the person who's making you feel that way."

Her eyes met his, wide and uncertain.

"I promise," she said quietly.

Jason reached over and squeezed her hand. *"Good."*

Outside, a gust of wind rattled the café's windowpane. Neither of them noticed.

————

Celeste sat in the driver's seat of her car, the engine off but her mind racing at full speed. The sterile chill of the 10 Legal conference room still clung to her clothes, as though the entire building had branded her with something she couldn't wash off. She hadn't spoken a word on her way out. Not to the receptionist. Not to her coworkers. Not even to the attorney who'd told her, with all the subtlety of a guillotine, that she was officially named in the Carter v. APEX Logistics lawsuit.

She blinked at the steering wheel, her eyes glassy. One hand clutched the folder of printed documents they'd handed her on the way out—her name circled in bold red at least five times.

"*I don't even know what this means,*" she whispered to no one.

Her phone buzzed in the cupholder. Reflexively, she reached for it, but it was just a calendar reminder for a client check-in that now felt like a joke. Celeste swiped it away and opened her recent calls.

She stared at Valerie's name.

She'll know what this means. She's been through this kind of stuff before. She'll explain. She'll... she'll fix it.

She hit dial.

It rang. Once. Twice.

Voicemail.

Her heart dropped. She tried again.

Voicemail.

Her lips parted in disbelief, as if the act of not picking up the phone was a betrayal in and of itself. Valerie always answered. Even during meetings, even on weekends. *Always.*

Celeste's eyes welled up. She leaned forward, resting her forehead against the steering wheel.

"Please pick up..." she whispered.

No callback. No text.

Just a hollow silence that made everything echo worse.

She sat up slowly, wiping at her cheek, and finally pressed the record button on her voicemail.

"Hey, Val... I just left the meeting. They—they said my name, Val. Like... officially. And no one looked surprised. Not one person." Her voice wavered. *"I don't know what's going on, but you said this wasn't anything to worry about. I—I'm trying to believe that. Just... call me, please?"*

She hung up and stared straight ahead through the windshield, where the world continued on as if her own hadn't just tilted. A woman pushed a stroller across the street. A delivery truck beeped as it backed into a loading dock. Normal life persisted. But inside her chest, something frayed was beginning to snap.

She leaned back, eyes closing, letting the silence swell around her.

The sound of a voicemail notification broke her reverie. She sighed, almost not wanting to listen, but the pull of curiosity was too strong. Maybe it was Valerie calling to check in, to reassure her that things would be okay.

"*Celeste,*" the voicemail began, Jason's familiar voice heavy with concern. "*I've been thinking about what you said the other night, and I really think you need to take a step back and look at the bigger picture. I know you've been through a lot with all of this legal stuff, but... just be careful who you trust, okay? There's more going on than you realize.*"

Celeste's chest tightened as Jason's words echoed in her mind. *Just be careful who you trust.* She could feel the weight of his warning settling in her stomach, but there was nothing she could do about it now. Everything was happening so fast, and she was drowning in a flood of confusion and pain.

The voicemail ended, but Celeste remained frozen in her seat, her eyes locked on the phone in her hands. *Who could she trust?* The thought felt like a lead weight in her chest.

She had spent so many years building her career on honesty, integrity, and hard work. She had never needed to second-guess anyone until now. And yet, as she sat there in the dim interior of her car, she couldn't shake the feeling that the ground beneath her was crumbling.

Her phone buzzed again. This time, it was a text from Valerie.

Valerie Henshaw: *"Celeste, are you okay? Please let me know if you need anything. I'm thinking of you."*

Celeste stared at the message. Her mind was too clouded to decipher it clearly, but the words, the sentiment—they felt like nothing more than hollow promises now. Did Valerie mean it? Was she really trying to help, or was this just another calculated move to keep Celeste close, to keep her under her thumb?

With shaking hands, Celeste tapped out a reply, her fingers fumbling over the keys.

Celeste Monroe: *"I'm just… trying to process everything. I'll reach out when I can."*

She sent the message and then stared at the screen for several long moments, wishing for the clarity that had always come so easily before.

But now, everything felt off-kilter. She couldn't trust herself anymore, let alone anyone else.

With a heavy sigh, Celeste wiped her eyes, took a deep breath, and started the car.

———

Valerie set her coffee mug on the coaster beside her keyboard, the steam curling upward like smoke from a candle just blown out. She had finally logged into her remote desktop system after spending the better part of the morning in her robe, shuffling from window to window in her quiet house. A soft instrumental playlist hummed from her smart speaker—low enough not to distract, but calming in that curated, intentional way she liked.

She felt better. Settled.

Celeste's voicemail had come through almost twenty minutes ago. Valerie hadn't listened to it all the way through. She didn't need to. The tremble in Celeste's voice during the first few seconds had told her everything she wanted to know.

She had considered calling back. Just to play the part. Offer a shoulder. Maybe even fake a few gasps and drop a *"That doesn't sound right"* or *"Let me look into it."* But she decided against it. Let Celeste squirm a little. Let her *need* her. That was always when Valerie had the most power — when people reached for her, not knowing the thorns beneath the lace.

Now, in the stillness of her home office, Valerie clicked into her inbox and began methodically purging old threads. She knew exactly which emails to delete: vendor communications, invoice trails, scheduling confirmations. It wasn't so much about hiding—she'd already covered her tracks months ago—but there was something satisfying about erasing it all now. Like sweeping confetti after a parade.

Her eyes flicked to a folder she'd labeled innocuously: *"APEX_Temp_Review."* Inside were renamed files, massaged spreadsheets, and one critical PDF she'd stolen from the shared network six weeks ago—the proprietary scoring matrix that could make or break a multi-million-dollar contract. The same one she had quietly fed to her *real* client, the one who'd promised her a healthy cut through a *"consulting"* agreement after retirement.

She opened the document briefly, letting her eyes drift across the numbers. It was almost poetic, the way everything lined up now. Celeste had been so concerned with doing things *"the right way,"* so invested in protocol and fairness. And look where it got her.

Valerie closed the file and sipped her coffee, smirking slightly.

People at work didn't like her, she knew that. They never said it out loud—not to her face, anyway. But she saw it in their eyes, in the subtle way conversations ended when she walked in. It didn't matter. She wasn't there to be liked. She was there to be remembered.

Celeste had always been the golden one. The woman others asked for by name. The one execs invited to lunch, the one HR called *"a shining example of leadership."*

Valerie had nearly vomited the first time she heard that.

She minimized the folder and opened a new browser tab. Her fingers flew over the keys as she logged into a private financial dashboard—one connected to her husband Nathan's business account. Another quiet corner where she'd been stashing small *"consulting deposits"* for nearly a year. Untouchable. Untraceable.

A soft vibration hummed across her desk—her phone again. Celeste.

Valerie glanced at it. Let it ring.

When it stopped, she smiled, stood, and stretched. The sky outside her window was bright and full of possibility.

———

The following day, Valerie glanced at the phone again as it lit up with Celeste's name for the second time in less than an hour. She let it vibrate its way to silence.

A moment later, she heard footsteps approaching from down the hall. Nathan appeared at the doorway, still in his workout clothes, towel slung around his neck, a smoothie in hand.

"*You're up and dressed,*" he said with a smile, clearly surprised. "*Wasn't sure if you were gonna stay horizontal all day after that meltdown last night.*"

Valerie chuckled softly, the way she always did when she wanted to seem composed. "*It wasn't a meltdown, Nate. It was just...a lot.*"

"*She called you again?*" he asked, nodding toward her buzzing phone.

Valerie shrugged and turned her chair slightly to face him. "*Yeah. Poor thing's spiraling. Everything's falling apart for her, and she's clinging to whoever answers. I'll call her later.*"

Nathan took a long sip of his smoothie. "*That's what I like about you. You've always got time for people, even when they don't deserve it.*"

Valerie raised her eyebrows and tilted her head, playing innocent. "*What's that supposed to mean?*"

He smiled. "*You know what I mean. You bend over backwards for folks like Celeste. Always have. Honestly, I don't know how she even got tangled up in this mess—she always seemed like a straight shooter.*"

Valerie let out a small sigh, carefully measured. "*Yeah... but even good people can make bad calls, right?*"

He nodded slowly, his brow furrowing with thought. "*True. Still sucks. You've helped her a lot over the years. I hope she doesn't try to drag you into it.*"

Valerie's eyes sparkled as she stood and walked toward him, smoothing a wrinkle from his shirt as she passed. "*She knows better than to do that. I've got everything buttoned up.*"

He kissed her on the forehead, content. "*That's my girl.*"

She watched him walk back down the hallway, her expression cooling the second he turned away. Her fingers tapped lightly against the side of her mug.

Everyone always thinks I'm the one they can count on, she thought. *Until they realize I was counting, too—just not for them.*

She returned to her desk, pulled up her secure email client, and began drafting a new message. She had three more steps before this thing could be wrapped. And the next phase? It would be the most rewarding of all.

CHAPTER SIX

BEHIND CLOSED DOORS

"The worst kind of lie is the one that pretends to be truth."
— Anonymous

SUNDAY AFTERNOON, 4:57 P.M.

The kitchen was quiet, save for the soft hum of the refrigerator and the rhythmic tap of Celeste's foot against the tile floor. A half-prepped cutting board sat untouched on the island, a bell pepper rolled to its edge as though it too had given up. Celeste stood by the stove with a wooden spoon in hand, staring at the pot of boiling water as if it held answers. It didn't.

She hadn't eaten all day, despite the gnawing in her stomach. The anxiety had taken root in her chest—a silent, pressing weight that refused to lift. Somewhere in the living room, her phone buzzed again. She didn't check it. Not anymore.

Her house, usually pristine, looked like it had been abandoned midweek. A laundry basket overflowed on the staircase, unread mail lay scattered across the coffee table, and a blanket had fallen to the floor, where it now lay bunched up like a forgotten thought. Her sanctuary had become a visual manifestation of her mind: cluttered, unsettled, unraveling.

Celeste finally turned off the burner and set the spoon down with a soft clack. She walked into the living room and sank into the couch, curling her legs beneath her. The silence in the house was deafening—not peaceful, but accusatory.

Out of habit, she reached for her phone and opened their old messages—*hers* and Valerie's. There were hundreds. Daily check-ins, prayers, scriptures, inside jokes. *"You're covered, friend." "God is with you, always." "You're doing amazing —don't let them dull your shine."* Words that once brought comfort now felt weaponized. Drenched in deceit.

She scrolled until her thumb ached, searching for something that might reveal the moment everything shifted. But of course, there was no smoking gun. Valerie had been too careful for that. All Celeste found were tiny inconsistencies she hadn't noticed before: advice that pulled her away from certain projects, suggestions that now seemed more like sabotage. A sudden gut feeling flickered—had she really been a pawn all along?

She tossed the phone aside and buried her face in her hands. A sound escaped her throat—not quite a sob, not quite a scream. Just grief in its rawest, most confusing form.

It wasn't just about the lawsuit. It was about the collapse of something sacred. Valerie had been a fixture in her life, a mentor, a spiritual sister, someone she had thanked God for in her prayers. And now?

Celeste's eyes landed on the bookshelf across the room. Tucked between two devotionals was an old journal. She reached for it and flipped it open to the last page her mother had written in—a shaky scrawl from hospice, dated two weeks before her passing.

"Be careful with women who wear masks, baby. Not every sweet voice is a kind one. Some people love you with half a heart — enough to keep you close, but never enough to truly protect you."

Celeste ran her fingers over the faded ink. A tear slipped down her cheek. She closed the journal gently, like it was something holy. The ache in her chest deepened.

She had been so sure. So certain of Valerie. Of God's hand in their friendship. But now, all of it felt like a lie.

She picked her phone up again. No new messages. Not from Valerie. Not from anyone. She opened the call log and stared at Jason's name. Hovered. Didn't press it.

Not yet.

The journal still rested in her lap, but Celeste had stopped looking at it. She stared at the wall ahead, numb. Even her tears had paused—as if her body, too, was taking a break from trying to make sense of everything.

Outside, the sun was beginning to set, casting warm amber light through the blinds. The shadows on the wall looked like prison bars. She'd always loved this time of day—the golden hour. Her mother used to call it *"God's spotlight."* A time to be still and listen.

But Celeste didn't feel God here now. She hadn't felt Him since the legal notice arrived.

She stood slowly and walked to the mirror above the fireplace. Her reflection startled her. Her eyes were swollen, her hair was frizzed, her skin dull. She looked like someone unraveling from the inside out. A ghost in her own home.

"How did I let this happen?" she whispered to herself. Her voice cracked mid-sentence, dry and unfamiliar. *"How did I not see it?"*

Her thoughts returned to Valerie's smile—always warm, always affirming. The way she'd touched Celeste's hand during prayer, the scriptures she'd texted during hard moments, the way she spoke of loyalty and faith like sacred oaths. Celeste had believed her. Had trusted her in rooms where trust was currency.

Now, it all felt corrupted.

She moved back to the couch and sat again, folding inward. Her phone buzzed with a calendar reminder. *"Weekly check-in with Valerie — 6:30 PM."* The irony gutted her. She canceled the reminder and deleted the recurring event. For a second, her finger hovered over Valerie's contact — *Valerie Henshaw | Faith Sister.*

She stared at it.

Then, almost gently, she edited the contact. Deleted the tagline. Left only the name.

A knock sounded faintly in the distance—a delivery at the front door. She ignored it. The outside world could wait. Right now, the wreckage inside her home, inside her heart, was enough to sit with.

Celeste curled tighter into the couch, pulled the blanket over her knees, and whispered a quiet prayer—not for strength, not for clarity. Just for something to hold onto.

Something real.

SUNDAY EVENING, 7:09 P.M.

The choir swayed gently, dressed in royal blue robes, their voices rising like incense through the sanctuary. Valerie stood among them, her arms outstretched, palms turned upward, a serene smile on her face as the final notes of *"He's Never Failed Me Yet"* filled the air.

She looked like peace incarnate—glowing under the soft cathedral lighting, eyes closed in solemn praise. Even her daughter, seated in the front pew beside Nathan, glanced up at her mother with admiration.

Valerie opened her eyes slowly as the congregation

applauded, nodding humbly, hand over heart as she stepped down from the risers. Pastor Melvin clasped her shoulder with fatherly affection. *"Beautiful as always, Sister Henshaw."*

"All glory to God," she replied smoothly. *"Just happy to serve."*

She took her seat beside Nathan, legs crossed neatly, bulletin folded on her lap. He leaned toward her, whispering, *"That was one of your best solos yet."*

"Spirit was moving today," she whispered back with a soft laugh. *"Guess He knows I need the strength."*

Nathan smiled, brushing her hand. *"Still worried about that thing at work?"*

"Mmhmm. But I think it'll work out fine," she said, voice sweet like honey. *"People just need to stay in their lane. That's all."*

Nathan didn't catch the undertone, but Valerie didn't expect him to. After all these years, he still thought she was the moral compass of their household. She didn't blame him. She played the part well.

As the sermon began, Valerie pulled out her leather-bound notebook—a prop, mostly—and jotted down the scripture of the day. *James 1:8 – A double minded man is unstable in all his ways.*

The irony almost made her laugh.

As Pastor Melvin spoke about truth and accountability, Valerie's mind drifted to her Outlook inbox. She'd have to delete a few more threads before Monday. And that older vendor invoice—the one Celeste forwarded last spring with the flagged discrepancy—she'd need to doctor that, too. Couldn't risk even a shadow of a trail.

Her gaze slid across the pews. Deaconess Temple was smiling at her—always impressed by Valerie's *"grace under pressure."* That's what people said. She was the one to call when someone needed calming, clarity, or conflict resolution.

They didn't know how many of those fires she'd started herself.

Her phone buzzed discreetly in her purse. She checked it under the cover of the bulletin. A new voicemail from Celeste.

She didn't open it.

Instead, Valerie closed her eyes again and mouthed a silent prayer—not for forgiveness, but for endurance. She was nearly on the other side of this.

By next quarter, the contract would be secured. Her friend would get the award. Her name would stay clean. Celeste would be discredited—professionally, legally, emotionally—and Valerie would emerge as the loyal one who *"tried to help."*

She pressed her hands together in a mock prayer, her voice a whisper in the quiet of her mind.

The sermon drew to a close. Pastor Melvin offered the benediction, arms raised in blessing: *"May the Lord bless you and keep you... May He make His face to shine upon you and give you peace."*

The congregation murmured their amens. The organ began its final chords as the members began to rise, smiling, embracing, exchanging next weekend plans and well wishes.

Valerie stood gracefully, smoothing the lines of her dress. She offered a warm hug to the pastor's wife and a few kind words about the floral arrangement near the altar. A shy teenager with tear-stained cheeks approached, nervously clutching a textbook under her arm.

"Midterms," the girl whispered. *"I don't think I'm gonna pass math."*

Valerie placed a gentle hand on her shoulder. *"Sweetheart, listen to me—the same God who gave Solomon wisdom is still handing it out. Pray before you study. Take deep breaths. You'll do just fine."*

The girl beamed.

As Valerie walked with her family toward the church doors, she smiled with ease, pausing to speak to Deaconess Temple, nod to Brother Warren in the tech booth, and wave at a toddler toddling between pews.

No one saw the calculation behind the smile. No one questioned the perfection.

They never did.

She walked outside into the crisp evening twilight and inhaled deeply, a quiet satisfaction rising in her chest. Everything was going according to plan.

She reached into her purse, silenced her phone without listening to the voicemail, and slipped her glasses on—created specifically for seeing things clearer when surrounded by darkness.

"You're almost there. Just hold on." She reminded herself.

SUNDAY NIGHT, 9:17 P.M.

The kitchen was dim, illuminated only by the soft, ambient light of the security lamps outside. Celeste sat at the breakfast table, arms wrapped around herself, legs tucked up into the oversized sweater she hadn't changed out of since Friday. Her phone lay screen-down beside a lukewarm cup of peppermint tea she'd made hours earlier but never drank.

All around her, the silence was heavy.

She'd spent most of the day trying to convince herself that everything would pass—that Valerie would call back, that some kind of clarification or explanation was coming. But no text arrived. No call. Just a void where friendship used to live.

Her laptop sat open nearby, her email inbox still pulled up. She had reread old threads from Valerie at least three times now, searching for anything she might've missed. Wording. Timing. Tone.

She reached for her phone again, scrolling through saved voicemails—the ones she couldn't bear to delete. Most were from work or random confirmations. Then she saw it.

"Mom – saved 2 years ago."

Her thumb hovered over the play button.

She wasn't sure why she clicked it. Maybe because she needed something familiar. Or maybe because her spirit was finally ready to hear something she hadn't let herself absorb before.

Her mother's voice crackled through the speaker, soft and warm like a favorite blanket on a bitter day:

"Hey baby... I know I already said this earlier, but I just needed to say it again. Be careful with people who only love you halfway. Folks will smile in your face and secretly resent your joy. Don't let your light make you blind, Celeste. Pay attention. The devil don't always come in horns."

Celeste's breath caught in her throat. Her mother had left that message the week she got promoted—the same week Valerie had taken her out to celebrate and told her how proud she was.

She'd laughed when she played this voicemail before. Thought it was just her mother being protective.

But now...

She pressed the phone to her chest and let the tears come.

Not just because of the lawsuit, or the money, or the silence. But because she was finally starting to realize that she had been walking through a relationship built on something that *wasn't real.* Something that only looked like love on the outside.

She rose slowly and walked into the living room. On the mantel sat a framed photo from a company banquet—Valerie and Celeste with arms linked, both smiling like sisters.

Celeste picked it up. Studied it.

Was she ever really my friend at all?

Her hands trembled slightly as she put the frame back in its place.

The truth wasn't just beginning to hurt.

It was beginning to take shape.

———

SUNDAY NIGHT, 9:17 P.M.

Valerie sat at her desk in the corner of her home office, fingers gliding smoothly across the keyboard as she sorted and renamed a series of documents. The soft glow of her desk lamp illuminated color-coded folders stacked with precision, each labeled and dated. She'd already cleared most of her work backlog by midafternoon, which left time tonight for more delicate tasks—like reviewing internal communications for anything that could be interpreted as implicating.

Her Spotify playlist hummed softly in the background—old gospel mixed with 90s R&B. A perfect balance of righteousness and nostalgia.

She took a long sip of her chamomile tea, satisfied.

Celeste still hadn't called again. Good. The silence meant the storm had reached her—and was now starting to work its way through her mind. Doubt, fear, isolation. Valerie knew the stages intimately. Once Celeste began to question herself, the others wouldn't be far behind.

A quiet ping sounded from her phone.

She glanced down: it was the group chat with her college girlfriends—sorors—a circle of women who'd grown up sharp, religious, and just petty enough to send sarcastic memes late on Sunday nights.

Valerie smirked as she read the one Jasmine had just sent.

It showed a cartoon woman ducking a flying Bible, with the caption:

"When your coworker wants to pray but she's the reason the buildings on fire."

Valerie laughed aloud. She could've sworn it had been *her* idea to use that metaphor first.

Without thinking, she tapped *Forward*, typed *"You dodging bullets this week too, sis?"* and hit send.

But the moment her thumb released the screen, something dropped in her stomach.

She hadn't double-checked the recipient.

Eyes wide, Valerie opened her messages.

The text had gone to *APEX Weekly Leads – Region D.* Her professional group chat. Not the girls.

Her heart slammed against her chest.

Four seconds passed. Then five.

Frantic, she pressed and held the message— *"Unsend"* glowed like a lifeline. She tapped it, breath locked in her throat. The message vanished.

She exhaled, slowly. Checked the timestamps. No one had reacted. No little *"Read"* bubbles. Maybe no one had seen it yet. Maybe God was still giving her one more chance to shut her mouth and stay clean.

She leaned back in her chair, blinking hard.

Focus. Tighten up. You're almost there.

Valerie stood, crossed the room, and looked at herself in the wall mirror near the bookshelf. Her reflection stared back, composed but winded. She smoothed a hand over her hair.

"You're too close to fumble now," she whispered.

Her voice didn't crack.

Her mask didn't move.

But deep behind her eyes, something flickered—not guilt exactly... but the recognition that the finish line was closer than it had ever been. And her margin for error? Paper-thin.

MONDAY, 1:48 P.M.

The elevator ride up to the third floor felt longer than usual. Celeste stood in the corner, arms crossed, her reflection distorted in the metal paneling. The hum of fluorescent lights above her buzzed in time with her headache.

She hadn't wanted to come in. She wasn't ready. But her badge still worked, and there had been no directive from HR or legal telling her to stay home. So she came.

Don't give them a reason to think you're unraveling.
That voice again. The one that had grown louder since Friday.

As the doors slid open, she forced herself to take a full breath and step out. Her heels clicked against the tile in slow, reluctant rhythm. She passed the marketing department's seasonal bulletin board—bright with autumn leaves and corny slogans like *"Change is Beautiful."*

Right.

She reached her office and paused at the door. Someone had left a manila envelope tucked beneath the handle. No name, no label. Just there.

Celeste reached down, picked it up, and quickly slid it into her workbag. She didn't open it. Not yet.

Inside, her office was untouched—as if nothing had shifted. Her coffee mug still sat by the monitor, a half-dead succulent leaned toward the window, and a sticky note on her whiteboard read *"Don't forget to submit T&A."*

She dropped her bag onto the chair and closed the door quietly behind her.

The silence was loud.

She stared at the computer screen for a long time before reaching for the mouse. Her hands were trembling again. Click by click, she opened her inbox. Over 100 unread emails—and more Teams notifications than she could process.

People still needed things from her. People were still moving forward.

But she wasn't. Not really.

Celeste sat down, opened a fresh notebook, and tried to make a to-do list—anything to ground herself.

Instead, she found herself staring at the edge of her desk. Right where Valerie had once perched during late-evening brainstorming sessions. Where she had sat, offering scripture and sisterhood. Where she had laughed.

Celeste swallowed hard. Her eyes burned.

The knock came gently. She stiffened.

"*Hey*," said a familiar voice—soft, a little hesitant. It was Tasha from compliance.

Celeste opened the door halfway. "*Hey.*"

"*I just wanted to… check on you. I know it's a lot right now. But if you ever need to talk—outside of work, I mean—I'm around.*"

Celeste tried to nod. Her smile didn't… "*Thank you.*"

Tasha gave her arm a gentle squeeze. *"You've got more people in your corner than you realize."*

The door shut again, and Celeste stood frozen for a beat. She leaned against the frame and whispered, *"Do I?"*

MONDAY, 2:26 P.M.

Valerie sat in her car just underneath the downtown library, laptop balanced on her knees, phone pressed between shoulder and cheek. She always parked three levels below ground when working off-site—no chance of coworkers seeing her, no chance of being tracked.

"Nathan, I'm fine," she said breezily. *"I just had to take care of a few emails and stop by the resource center for that volunteer thing."* She smiled, even though he couldn't see her. *"You know how I am. Always doing the most."*

She ended the call and immediately tapped open the secure messaging app she'd installed months ago. *Just in case.*

A name lit up the screen: **T. Griffin – Regional Strategy**.

She read the incoming message twice.

> *"Did you see the list? Monroe was added last minute. You good?"*

117

Valerie paused, fingers hovering above the keyboard. *Think. Don't respond too quickly.*

She typed back:

> *"I saw. It's unfortunate, but not unexpected. I hope she has a strong legal team."*

Then, as if to exhale her own anxiety, she minimized the app and opened her personal email. There, in a folder marked *Receipts*, were screenshots, email chains, and redacted notes—carefully curated breadcrumbs of *"truth,"* some real, some bent. All useful, if the heat ever turned toward her.

She had already contacted HR the previous week, under the guise of *"ethical compliance concerns."* The narrative she built was slow but intentional—suggesting that she had *suspected mismanagement for months* but had been too loyal to speak up. Her language was always cautious, her paper trail meticulous.

In the same folder, she kept another set of notes: her exit plan. The names of contacts at a few competing firms. Quiet feelers sent out through LinkedIn. A draft of a resignation letter that said nothing but looked polished.

She'd made it this far.

Her pulse slowed as she took a sip from the thermos she always brought with her—black coffee, two drops of almond extract, just the way she liked it. The ritual made her feel powerful.

Another notification:

Calendar Invite – "10-Min Touch Base: Valerie + HR"

She smirked.

Perfect timing.

Valerie glanced up at her reflection in the rearview mirror. Lipstick still perfect. Eyes calm. No one would guess.

She adjusted her blouse, smoothed down a flyaway curl, and whispered to herself, *"You're almost there. Keep moving."*

Then she closed the laptop with a soft click and backed out of the parking spot like nothing was on fire.

———————

TUESDAY MORNING – 12:48 A.M.

Celeste lay sprawled on top of the covers, still fully dressed, one heel kicked off, the other dangling from her toes. The soft hum of the air conditioning was the only sound in the room, but inside her chest, everything felt loud. Her thoughts raced in endless loops.

The house, usually a sanctuary, had taken on a strange hollowness. Lights dimmed in most rooms, the flicker from the muted television across the room cast shadows against the wall. She hadn't watched a single scene.

Her phone buzzed. She lunged toward it, hope flaring—maybe Valerie had finally called her back.

But it was just a promotional email. Junk.

She sank back into the pillows, arms flung across her eyes. Her body was drained, but her mind wouldn't stop. Every scene played again in her head—the conference room, the lawsuit, Valerie's absence, the unanswered calls, Jason's warning.

Was she ever really my friend?

She rolled over and stared at the ceiling, where a lazy fan spun in slow, hypnotic circles. Somewhere in the silence, she heard the soft tick of the wall clock. She thought of her mother again —of how she used to say, *"The enemy doesn't always arrive in red. Sometimes, it comes dressed in Sunday white."*

That phrase hit different now.

She sat up and reached for her laptop.

If she couldn't sleep, maybe she could *do* something. Something productive. Something to make her feel in control again.

But the screen stared back at her blankly, the blinking cursor feeling like mockery. She opened her inbox, scrolled through old messages from Valerie. So many of them ended with phrases like, *"Always here for you"* or *"Just trust me."*

Her eyes burned.

The cursor blinked.

She closed the laptop.

By 3:06 a.m., she was curled on the floor at the foot of her bed, wrapped in a throw blanket, holding a pillow like a life raft. Silent tears traced the same worn path down her cheeks. Sleep never came—only that gnawing ache of confusion, anger, and heartbreak.

TUESDAY MORNING – 6:42 A.M.

Valerie stood in front of the mirror, tugging a thin gold hoop through her left ear with steady hands. The early morning sun poured in through the tall windows of her en suite bathroom, glinting off the marble counter, illuminating her flawless complexion and the soft waves she'd carefully styled into her hair.

She adjusted her blouse—ivory silk, modest neckline, just the right pop of class. Understated. Deliberate.

Her reflection stared back: polished, composed, unbothered.

Her phone pinged beside her sink.

It was a news alert about the Carter case—public now. She didn't flinch. She'd known the timeline. She'd orchestrated the timeline.

She tapped the screen once to clear it, then picked up her lipstick.

In the distance, Nathan's voice called out—something about the coffee being ready. Valerie responded sweetly, assuring him she'd be down in a moment.

She liked mornings like this. Quiet. Predictable. Controlled.

And more importantly, mornings where *she* was winning.

Her eyes drifted to the far corner of the mirror, where a small, framed quote sat beside a faux floral arrangement:

"The heart is deceitful above all things..."

She smirked.

That one had always made her laugh.

Because in her mind, it wasn't deceit. It was strategy. Self-preservation. Survival. Celeste never understood that—never learned how the world *really* worked.

Valerie leaned in closer to the mirror, inspecting the liner along her upper lash.

"You've done well," she whispered to her reflection, soft and sure. *"You've outsmarted them all."*

A knock on the door. Her daughter's voice chirped through it: *"Mom, where's my choir binder?"*

Valerie didn't break her gaze from the mirror. She took one more look—a long, self-satisfied one—then turned off the bathroom light.

She walked away without answering.

———

CHAPTER SEVEN

CRACKS IN THE ARMOR

"There is nothing concealed that will not be disclosed, or hidden that will not be made known."
— Luke 12:2 (NIV)

WEDNESDAY MORNING — APEX LOGISTICS, 9:02 A.M.

Celeste sat in the HR conference room, posture straight, hands folded tightly in her lap. Her blouse—ivory silk, once a statement of elegance—now clung to her skin like a second layer of anxiety. The air in the room felt dense. Two chairs away, a junior HR rep fumbled with the speakerphone, while Patricia Langston, Director of Employee Relations, adjusted her glasses with the kind of calm that only came from decades of watching other people's careers burn quietly.

"Before we begin," Patricia said, her voice even, *"I want to acknowledge that this is a stressful time. We are here to be transparent about what's required of you now that APEX has*

been formally subpoenaed in the Carter v. APEX Logistics matter."

Celeste nodded, though she felt like her spine might snap from the tension.

A third person entered the room—a man from the Legal Risk and Compliance team. She didn't catch his name. She barely caught anything after that.

They laid it out plainly: she was not being terminated, but she would be expected to cooperate fully. She was being named in the lawsuit not as a random party, but as someone who had *"touched key data related to the awarded contract."* If her name appeared on a chain of approvals, the plaintiff's attorneys would dig. If she attended meetings, signed documents, or even replied *"looks good"* in an email, it would be scrutinized.

Celeste felt her stomach twist.

"We will be forwarding the subpoena to your personal counsel," Patricia continued.

She blinked. *"My... personal counsel?"*

"We recommend that you retain an attorney as soon as possible," the man from Legal added. *"You have the right to independent representation. APEX cannot advise you, nor will our corporate counsel represent you personally in this matter."*

Just like that, the company she'd bled for—working overtime, mentoring junior analysts, volunteering for every miserable

Friday closeout—had drawn a dotted line around her name. *You are on your own now.*

As she signed a form acknowledging the conversation, Celeste noticed Patricia glance quickly toward the camera in the corner of the ceiling. It was always watching. Everything she did from now on would be examined through a legal lens.

And yet, not once did they mention Valerie Henshaw.

As the HR interview began winding down, a junior HR staffer —nervously flipping through a thin manila folder—muttered something almost under her breath. *"Weird... Valerie was cc'd on the September 12 chain, but your name's not in here until the forward two weeks later."*

Celeste blinked. *"I'm sorry—what chain?"*

The staffer looked up, startled. *"Oh—it's probably nothing. Just an old vendor discussion. Legal's got it now."*

But it wasn't nothing. Celeste's mind immediately latched onto it. If there had been a string of conversations involving Valerie —and not her—about a matter Celeste was supposedly leading, why hadn't she seen it? Why was she added two weeks later?

———

WEDNESDAY — 10:47 A.M. | APEX LOGISTICS, PRIVATE FOCUS ROOM

The hallway outside HR felt cold, sterile. Celeste didn't even make it back to her desk. She ducked into an empty focus room, closed the door, and stood there, her hand still trembling from signing the company's legal notice.

She'd never had to hire a lawyer before. Hell, she'd never even *needed* one. She wasn't that kind of person. Or so she thought.

Her phone buzzed in her hand. Jason had replied to her voicemail from Sunday:

> *"Call me when you can. I'll walk you through whatever you need."*

She hesitated.

Jason had always been honest with her—sharp, grounded, observant. He wasn't flashy, and he never pushed his opinions. But still… a part of her recoiled.

Valerie had been honest, too. Until she wasn't.

Celeste stared at the message. Even trusting people felt like a risk now.

She sent him a quick text:

> *"I'm about to call. HR just told me I need a lawyer. Do you know anyone good?"*

He called her immediately. His voice was calm, low, steady.

"I've got a guy," he said. *"He's in midtown. Bit expensive, but he's sharp and discreet. Benjamin Croft. He's good. I've used him before for something I can't really get into, but trust me— he knows how to handle sensitive messes like this."*

Celeste scribbled down the name: *Benjamin Croft, Attorney at Law.* "Thanks," she said, voice flat. *"I... I'll check him out."*

"Hey," Jason said gently. *"I know you're second-guessing everything right now. That's normal. Do your research. But don't wait too long. These things move fast."*

Jason's voice dipped lower near the end of the call.

"Look, I've been talking to someone who used to be at APEX... someone Valerie used to work with years ago, back when she was over at Field Ops."

Celeste leaned into the phone, her hand clutching the back of her neck.

"She said Valerie was... strategic. Nice to your face, but always moving pieces behind the scenes."

He hesitated. *"There was something Valerie said to her recently. About a situation with you—not in detail, but enough that it felt... off."*

Celeste's stomach turned.

129

Jason's voice softened. *"I'm going to send you something. Just look at it. When you're ready."*

Instantly, Celeste realized: Jason had started to doubt Valerie, too.

"Thanks, Jason."

She hung up, but didn't call Croft right away.

Instead, she opened her laptop and started Googling:
'best employment defense attorneys near me.'
'civil litigation firms for corporate disputes.'
'lawyers for employees named in workplace lawsuit.'

Firm after firm popped up, with gleaming testimonials and photos of smiling partners in sleek suits. She called three of them.

The first said they were unavailable until next week. The second quoted a $7,500 retainer—nonrefundable. The third redirected her to an intake coordinator who seemed more interested in whether her company had *"insurance that might reimburse the cost."*

By 12:15, her head ached.

Her fingers hovered over Jason's contact again.

She hadn't wanted to take his advice. She hadn't wanted to trust *anyone*. But the truth was, she was unraveling—and no amount of internet research or stiff professionalism could stop it.

She dialed Croft's office. A sharp-voiced receptionist answered.

"Yes, we have availability for a 30-minute consultation this afternoon at 3:30. Standard retainer is $4,000, with a minimum balance of $2,000 in trust at all times. We will email you a client intake form and conflict waiver."

Celeste closed her eyes.

Her voice cracked as she whispered into the phone. *"That's fine. Book me."*

WEDNESDAY – 12:17 P.M.

Celeste ended the call and laid her phone flat on the desk.

Four thousand dollars. Gone. Just like that.

She leaned back in the chair and closed her eyes, letting out a long, quiet breath. Her chest still felt tight, but something had shifted. The floor wasn't steady—not by a long shot—but she'd at least found footing.

This was life now. Legal representation. Financial strain. Reputation on the line.

She opened her eyes and stared at the ceiling, lips moving silently as she offered up a prayer. It wasn't poetic or formal—just raw.

"God... I didn't ask for this. I didn't cause this. But You've always taken care of me, and I trust You will again. I have to believe You will again."

She sat up straighter and reached for a notepad from the small supply drawer beside her. In neat script, she scribbled:

"$50,000 — max spend. If I have to fight this, I'll fight it smart."

It was a line in the sand. Fifty thousand dollars. Not a penny more.

She could do that. It would hurt, yes—but she had savings. A cushion. God had been generous to her, had *positioned* her well. Even in the middle of this chaos, she saw that. **Her bills were paid. She had a roof over her head. She had options.**

And she wasn't going to lose it all over a lie.

She gathered her things, tucked the notepad into her bag, and stepped out of the focus room. Her heels clicked softly on the tile floor as she headed toward the parking garage. She needed time, space, and maybe a drive with no destination.

But in her chest, a new resolve had taken root.

———

WEDNESDAY – 12:47 P.M.

Valerie adjusted the blinds in her office so the sunlight hit just right — warm but not glaring, golden but not overexposed. She preferred everything in moderation: light, tone, language, reactions. Especially reactions.

The email to the compliance team was already drafted. She'd spent the better part of an hour massaging the language until it sounded cooperative but oblivious. Professional, yet concerned. Informed, but not alarmed.

> *Hi Patricia,*
>
> *I wanted to follow up on any documentation you might need from me regarding the Carter matter. I understand there may be some confusion about timelines, so I've pulled what I have and am happy to make myself available for questions. Please advise if you'd like to meet in person or via Teams.*
>
> *Warmly,*
> *Valerie Henshaw*

She re-read it twice more before hitting send. Then, with practiced calm, she clicked into her project folders and began organizing the remaining evidence she *didn't* plan to share. She kept multiple storage locations—one for show, and one for real. The real one stayed on an external drive labeled "*Hannah's 5th Grade Projects.*" No one ever questioned the maternal folder names.

She opened her encrypted notes and reviewed a list of dates—emails she'd sent, conversations she'd steered, chain-of-command narratives she'd been subtly building for months. She deleted two calendar entries that would contradict her current story and edited one to make it look like a client call had come from Celeste's extension.

A clean story sells itself.

Nathan poked his head into the office, holding a coffee in each hand. *"Hey, I picked up an extra latte. Figured you'd be running on fumes."*

Valerie smiled so warmly you could toast bread with it. *"You're a saint. Thank you."*

He stepped in and set the cup down beside her keyboard. *"You holding up okay?"*

She tilted her head and gave a soft chuckle. *"As much as anyone can. This whole situation just blindsided us all. I feel so terrible for Celeste."*

Nathan nodded slowly, his brows drawn just enough to suggest sympathy. *"Yeah. Wild stuff."*

Valerie lowered her eyes and tapped her pen against the desk in a thoughtful rhythm. *"You know, she was always so driven. So brilliant. It's just... heartbreaking. I hope she has someone advising her well."*

A masterstroke of faux concern.

Nathan gave a half-shrug, then backed away toward the hallway. *"Let me know if you need anything."*

"I will. And thank you again for the coffee."

Once alone, Valerie sipped the latte and smirked softly into the lid. *"Showtime,"* she whispered.

She double-clicked a folder titled *Q2 Financials – Vendor Review* and opened a spreadsheet no one had actually requested. It was a decoy, open on her screen in case someone walked in.

But her real work was already done—tucked away, encrypted, scrubbed. She'd spent years mastering the art of plausible deniability. And now, with Celeste spinning and scrambling, the advantage had shifted entirely into her hands.

Her phone buzzed. A message from her daughter's piano teacher. Valerie responded quickly, kindly.

Another message buzzed in—this one from her pastor's wife:

"Thinking of you today. Love you, sis."

Valerie typed back:

"Love you more. God is still on the throne."

She hit send and sat back, fully content.

No one suspected a thing.

Not even Nathan.

Just then, her desk phone rang. A call from the APEX office.

They exchanged niceties and Valerie confirmed some information. Then the compliance officer, Rhonda, paused just before hanging up the call.

"Hey, Valerie — quick thing. Do you know where the vendor backup file is for Quarter 2? The email says Celeste drafted it, but the version uploaded doesn't follow her normal layout."

Valerie's jaw clenched for the briefest second—but she smiled. *"Oh — yeah. I think she was out that day and asked me to upload it on her behalf. I'll track it down and send it over."*

Rhonda thanked her and hung up.

Valerie sat frozen for a beat too long. She knew Celeste hadn't asked her anything of the sort. She'd intercepted the file— rewritten it slightly—just enough to make sure nothing pointed back to her.

But now? The small inconsistencies were being noticed.
She stood up and walked to the bathroom mirror, splashing water on her face.

"It's fine," she whispered to her reflection. *"You're still in control."*

But her eyes—for the first time in weeks—looked tired.

WEDNESDAY – 3:29 P.M.
CROFT LAW FIRM, MIDTOWN

The elevator chimed softly as Celeste stepped into the eleventh-floor lobby of the Croft Law Firm. She tightened her grip on the leather handle of her tote bag, the sound of her heels absorbed by the thick carpet beneath her. The waiting area was quiet, minimalist—brushed brass fixtures, walnut paneled walls, soft instrumental jazz curling through the space like incense. A trio of well-worn but expensive-looking chairs framed a small coffee table stacked with legal journals and design magazines.

The receptionist smiled at her with professional warmth. *"Ms. Monroe? Welcome to Croft. They're expecting you."*

Celeste offered a small smile and nodded, but inside, her nerves were fraying.

She had barely slept the night before. Her stomach was still tight from the HR meeting that morning, and she could still hear the junior staffer's offhand remark about the email chain —the one she had never seen. The one Valerie had somehow been cc'd on.

Her palms felt damp. She curled them discreetly against the lining of her coat.

When the intake coordinator arrived—a tall woman named Sasha with a calming voice and an impeccable suit—Celeste stood. They exchanged a quick greeting, and Sasha led her down a hallway lined with framed photos of smiling legal teams and high-profile case plaques. The entire place exuded quiet confidence, as though it had been built brick-by-brick to whisper, *You're safe here.*

The consultation room was bright and private, with a long table, legal pads stacked neatly, and a tray of bottled water. Two attorneys entered soon after—one mid-50s, silver-haired and serene, the other a younger partner with sharp eyes and the kind of clear diction that made juries lean in. They introduced themselves—*Dean Croft* and *Dana Marcene*—and made it clear from the outset: they had read her intake documents, were familiar with the case name *Carter v. APEX Logistics*, and believed she was smart to get ahead of it.

"People wait too long," Dean said, clasping his hands on the table. *"You didn't. That speaks volumes."*

For the first time in days, Celeste felt something close to relief.

She listened carefully, took notes, asked questions—lots of them. They answered patiently, without condescension, giving her room to breathe between sentences. Dana pulled up a copy of the public filing and walked her through the likely timeline. Dean, meanwhile, emphasized that while discovery would be time-intensive, he saw *"nothing in the initial allegations that pointed directly to misconduct"* on her part.

"And if we're smart and fast," Dana added, *"there's a path to settlement here. You might walk away under fifty."*

Celeste blinked. *"Fifty...?"*

"Thousand," Dean clarified. *"I know that sounds like a lot, but in legal terms, it's light. Especially for civil litigation of this type. We've seen companies settle for six times that to avoid PR fallout."*

She nodded, slowly. Fifty thousand. That's what she had committed to mentally already. If that was all it took to clear her name, then so be it.

Her chest loosened—just a little.

She let her pen rest against the edge of her notebook and took in the room again. These weren't ambulance chasers. They weren't sloppy. They were, for lack of a better word, *reassuring.* They made her believe she could fight this—not with bitterness, but with precision. With grace.

"Let's move forward," she said finally, her voice steady. *"Let's do it."*

They discussed terms: a $4,000 retainer, and a minimum $2,000 to be held in the coffer at all times. She signed the engagement letter before leaving—her hand steady, her resolve firmer than it had been in weeks.

As Sasha walked her back to the lobby, Celeste glanced at the skyline through the wide glass windows. The sun had finally emerged, breaking through the clouds in long golden fingers. *God had made provision. She could do this.*

What she didn't know—what she couldn't know—was that while she stood in that quiet lobby, grateful for the glimpse of hope, someone else was busy, laying the groundwork for her fall.

WEDNESDAY – 3:29 P.M.

Valerie sat in her car in the parking garage, the engine idling low beneath the quiet hum of gospel music. Her phone was in her lap, unlocked, but untouched. The email message from Rhonda had come through half an hour ago: a polite, routine follow-up on the missing backup file from last quarter's vendor audit.

Valerie's jaw tightened, per usual.

She hadn't expected anyone to circle back. Not this soon, anyway.

She inhaled deeply, smoothed her collar, then reached for her laptop from the passenger seat. If Rhonda was asking, others might follow—which meant she couldn't afford even the *appearance* of sloppiness. A new lie would need to be crafted.

One that felt so ordinary, so *boring*, no one would ever think to question it.

By the time she made it upstairs to her home office, Valerie had a plan. She pulled up an old, unused audit template and made small, intentional tweaks—enough to mimic Celeste's style, but not so perfect it would draw suspicion. Then she drafted an email, backdated it using a third-party client she'd used for years in her freelance nonprofit work.

She opened a second tab, created a draft of a follow-up message to herself with a fake attachment—a ZIP folder containing nothing but dummy PDFs.

In her reply to Rhonda, she played it clean:

> *"Hey Rhonda —*
>
> *Just saw your message. I remember Celeste emailed me that file weeks ago. I think I saved a copy locally just in case. Attaching here — let me know if anything's missing.*
>
> *Hope your day is going smoother than mine. :-)*
>
> *– Val"*

Then she sent it.

She sat back, exhaled. The mask never slipped.

Rhonda responded quickly:

"Perfect, thank you! We're good on our end.
Appreciate the quick turnaround."

Valerie smiled. It wasn't pride. It was relief—the kind of cold, strategic relief that came from knowing she was still ahead.

And still, that wasn't enough.

She opened her work chat and began sowing the next layer of distance.

> **Valerie Henshaw to Darlene Young**
> *"Hey — just a heads up, there's been a bit of*
> *confusion over that vendor audit file. I think Celeste*
> *may have sent it to the wrong distribution list initially,*
> *which is probably why Rhonda didn't see it. I cleaned*
> *it up and resent just to be safe."*

She left the message there like a breadcrumb—subtle, plausible. Nothing that accused. Just enough to plant the thought: Celeste might not be quite as buttoned-up as people thought.

A few moments later, Darlene responded with a thumbs-up emoji and a casual,

"Thanks, Val. Appreciate you staying on top of it!"

Valerie leaned back in her chair and let her fingers steeple under her chin.

Good.

By the time they figure out what really happened—*if* they figure it out—the narrative will already be shaped. And it won't be her name on anyone's lips.

She glanced over at the framed photo on her bookshelf—her, Nathan, and Madison at last year's harvest festival. Her smile in the photo was wide, luminous, flawless.

The image of a woman with nothing to hide.

WEDNESDAY – 11:03 P.M.

Celeste stared at the vendor audit document Jason had sent her. There—on the second page—was something unmistakable. A line break formatting style she always used when drafting documents. A double-dash header with a soft indent—a little quirk she picked up years ago.

But this wasn't a document she remembered writing.

Her hands trembled as she zoomed in.

The body of the email that contained the attachment listed her as the preparer—but the timestamps didn't match her calendar at all.

She hadn't written this. She was sure of it.

Her pulse raced.

She might not understand the full picture yet—but finally, she had something.

She sat curled on the far end of her sectional couch, one leg tucked under her and the other dangling off the edge, toes brushing the rug she used to love. The house was quiet—not peaceful, just silent in that heavy, oppressive way that made every breath feel loud. Even the hum of the refrigerator seemed to mock her.

Her phone sat face down on the coffee table, Jason's contact still at the top of her call log. The appointment was complete. A $4,000 retainer, $2,000 minimum in the trust. She had agreed. She had done what needed to be done.

And yet, she couldn't stop shaking.

"I can afford fifty," she whispered to herself. Her own voice felt foreign in the dark. *"I can give fifty. That's doable. God gave me enough cushion. I can handle this."*

She said it like a mantra, as if repeating it would turn it into truth.

She believed in God's provision. She did.

She had always donated. She had always helped others. She had always trusted.

But tonight, even her faith felt shaky.

She pulled the throw blanket tighter around her and stared at the ceiling. A faint water spot was forming near one of the vents—she made a mental note to call someone about it. Maybe next week. Maybe never.

Her eyes stung. Not from crying—that had already happened. That had passed. This was something else. Something more disorienting than tears.

Grief. Betrayal. Exhaustion.

She grabbed her laptop and opened it, searching for emails with the word "*compliance*." Then "*Carter*." Then "*Valerie*."

She read and reread.

Nothing obvious.

Nothing explosive.

Just... lines. Words. The same Valerie she had trusted, baked banana bread with, prayed with, cried with—signing her emails with "*Blessings*" and slipping in verses like she was born to uplift.

Celeste slammed the laptop shut. Her breathing came faster now.

"*How?*" she whispered. "*How could you?*"

The question wasn't even directed outward. It was collapsing inward—how could *she* not have seen it? How had she missed the signs?

She stood up and walked into the kitchen, hands moving almost automatically. She turned on the kettle and opened the cabinet for tea. Chamomile. Peppermint. Something with lavender.

But even her tea tasted off tonight. Everything did.

When she sat back down, the house still hadn't made a sound.

No messages.

No calls.

No word from Valerie.

Celeste blinked slowly, exhaustion pooling behind her eyes. Her hands clenched in her lap—she hadn't even realized she was gripping the fabric of her pants until her knuckles went white.

She took a breath.

Then another.

And finally—like something inside her had run out of power—she let herself fall sideways on the couch and whispered the only thing left she could trust:

"God... I'm still here. I'm scared, but I'm still here."

Her eyes fluttered closed. Sleep didn't come easy. But eventually, it came.

———

THURSDAY – 9:17 A.M.

Valerie sat at her desk in her home office, a mug of lemon tea growing cold beside her. The sun filtered in through the blinds, casting stripes of light across her sleek white workspace. She wore her favorite powder-blue blouse—the one with the pearl buttons—and a soft pink lip, just enough to say, *I'm approachable, but polished.*

On the screen in front of her was a carefully composed email draft. The subject line was bland: "**Follow-Up: Carter Matter.**" But the body was anything but casual.

Hi Janice,

Hope all is well. I just wanted to reiterate my full cooperation and transparency regarding the Carter situation. I've gone through my files and have no documentation outside of what's already been submitted. If anything changes or new information surfaces, I'll be sure to loop you in immediately.

Thanks again for handling everything with grace. These things are never easy, but I trust in the process. Let me know if there's anything else you need from me.

Valerie

She read it three more times, tweaking a word here, removing a period there. Perception was everything. She wasn't panicking —not outwardly. In fact, she was flourishing in the chaos. The Carter situation had rattled many, but not Valerie. Valerie, as usual, seemed serene.

She clicked send.

Then opened Slack.

In her HR channel, she posted a benign update about scheduling midyear performance reviews. In another group chat —one with a few managers from APEX's West Region—she dropped a line that sounded helpful but was deliberately vague:

> *"Let's all stay aligned as we navigate the compliance questions. Everyone has a part to play in ensuring we uphold the standards.*
>
> *Trust but verify, right?"*

She didn't mention Celeste. She didn't have to.

She knew the message would land exactly where it needed to. The West Region team was tight-knit, and rumors moved faster than memos. People would fill in the blanks. They always did.

Nathan walked in, holding his phone, grinning. *"Guess what? Madison's teacher emailed. She aced her science project. Best in class."*

Valerie's face lit up. *"Of course she did! I told her that robotic kit was going to be a hit."*

She stood and kissed his cheek, smoothly folding herself back into the rhythm of domestic life—the kind of life people trusted. The kind that made people say things like *Valerie? No way. She's solid. She's got a family. She volunteers. She sings in the choir.*

Nathan glanced at her screen, then casually asked, *"Everything good at work?"*

Valerie smiled. *"Just the usual shuffle. A lot of noise right now. But I'm staying out of the weeds."*

He nodded. *"Smart."*

Valerie turned back to her desk as he left the room, the warmth leaving with him. She stared at the Slack chat, then her inbox, then the top drawer where her work journal sat—the one with notes scribbled in shorthand that no one else would understand.

She opened it.

Flipped to a page dated three months ago.

"If this falls apart, distance quickly. Stay warm, not defensive."

She traced the words with her finger and whispered, "*And that's exactly what I'm doing.*"

Then she closed the journal and reached for her tea, now lukewarm, but still useful.

———

CHAPTER EIGHT

THE BEGINNING OF THE END

"The worst part about being lied to is knowing you weren't worth the truth."
— Jean-Paul Sartre

THURSDAY – 8:12 A.M.
LOCATION: CELESTE'S HOME OFFICE

Celeste sat on the edge of her office chair, still wearing the navy-blue satin robe she'd barely taken off all week. Her laptop chimed with a soft alert—the APEX remote work drive had finished syncing.

She hadn't opened her synced project folders since going on leave. Until now.

On her desktop was a neatly organized set of folders. She double-clicked one she hadn't thought about in months:

Vendor_Contracting_Q1. It was buried three levels deep inside another shared drive. It hadn't even crossed her mind when the lawsuit was filed.

Inside, there were eight documents. Most were templates and draft agreements. But one file stopped her cold: **CM_VendorRevised_Feb18_FINAL.docx**

Her initials.

Her formatting style.

But she hadn't worked that week.

She clicked it open. A wave of nausea rolled over her before she even read a word. It was written in her tone—the phrasing was close. It looked like her voice. But not quite.

There were formatting details that gave it away:

- The closing salutation was double spaced—she never did that.
- The margin spacing was slightly wider than her default style.
- And the metadata... the document history had been scrubbed.

A tightness formed behind her eyes. Not a headache—a kind of pressure that made her ears ring. She whispered to no one, "*I didn't write this.*"

The file had been uploaded by a user ID she didn't recognize. One she'd never seen before. She jotted it down:

"vh-temp-support3"

The initials hit her like a slow slap.

VH. Valerie Henshaw.

But Valerie didn't use temporary accounts. Unless...

Celeste closed the laptop lid with a trembling hand. Her stomach was in knots. For a second, she stood still, trying to breathe.

Her mind chased itself in circles.

Maybe someone saved it wrong. Maybe she edited something I started. Maybe it's all nothing.

But she knew better.

The only reason this version even existed was because someone wanted it to.

The kettle shrieked on the stove, but Celeste didn't move. She sat at the kitchen table, elbows propped against its edge, head in her hands. The house was silent except for the hum of the fridge and the faint ticking of the wall clock.

She'd been like this for hours. No makeup. No earrings. Just her robe and a growing sense of dread.

She had always believed that grief moved in stages—neat little sections of mourning like rooms in a hallway. But this wasn't neat. It was jagged and relentless, like waves crashing at irregular intervals.

And...This wasn't grief about her mother. That grief had been real, raw, and sacred. This was something else.

This was the grief of realizing she had trusted the wrong person.

The grief of betrayal.

The kettle clicked off behind her. Still, she didn't move.

Her phone vibrated across the table with a text from Jason:

"Thinking about you. Call if you need to."

She stared at it, then pressed her fingers to her forehead. Jason. He had always told her the truth. Valerie had told her what she wanted to hear.

There was a difference, and now Celeste could feel it in her bones.

She got up slowly and poured hot water over a chamomile tea bag, the scent wrapping around her like a memory. Her mother used to make her tea like this when life got too loud.

She turned toward the bay window and watched the trees sway.

She remembered a verse Valerie once quoted when Celeste was in hospice hell with her mom:

"God is not the author of confusion..."

And yet—confusion was all that remained now.

If not Valerie, she thought, *then who?*

But her heart already knew the answer.

FRIDAY – 1:18 P.M.
LOCATION: IN HER CAR OUTSIDE A SANDWICH SHOP

The kettle had shrieked on the stove yesterday, but Celeste hadn't moved. Not at first. She'd sat there at the kitchen table for hours—robe-clad, barefaced, hands in her hair, trying to gather the energy to stand.

That had been Thursday.

Today was Friday. Different clothes, same weight. She hadn't gone in to work. Hadn't answered emails. Had barely slept.

Now she was sitting in her car, engine off, parked outside the corner sandwich shop she used to frequent with Valerie—back before everything shifted.

Her stomach growled, but the idea of food made her nauseous.

She held the paper bag loosely in her lap. The sandwich inside —turkey, tomato, light mayo—remained untouched. She'd ordered it out of habit. The kind of meal you reach for when you're trying to tell your body, *See? Everything's fine.*

But nothing was fine.

She outstretched her hand and turned off the radio. Static had crept into the jazz station, and even the soft saxophone had started to feel like too much.

Her phone lit up with a new voicemail. Unknown number, but she recognized the area code. She played it on speaker, hand hovering near the volume button:

> *"Hi Ms. Monroe, this is Amanda with the Croft Law Group, calling on behalf of Mr. Croft. We're moving into discovery, and we'll need you to start compiling*

any and all communications related to the workstreams named in the suit—that includes emails, attachments, calendar invites, Teams chat records, client notes, anything pertaining to Phase 2 of the rollout. I've sent over a secure upload link and checklist. Let us know if you have any questions. We're here to walk with you through the process."

The message ended. The phone screen dimmed.

Celeste blinked slowly and leaned her head back against the headrest. Her throat tightened.

Discovery.

That word made it feel like this was really happening now. That this wasn't just a misunderstanding or an HR hiccup or a nightmare she could journal her way out of.

This was the beginning of unearthing every digital breadcrumb tied to a project she thought had been buttoned-up and buried. She had moved on from it. She thought they all had.

Her fingers curled tighter around the paper bag in her lap until the corners wrinkled.

This felt like a funeral. But for what?

Her career? Her peace? Her relationship with Valerie?

Her breath hitched. Her chest ached with something sharp and heavy.

She thought of all the scripture Valerie used to quote. All the nights they'd talked about hope and forgiveness and trusting God's plan. The prayer texts. The way Valerie would grip her hand, eyes shining, and say *"We're in this together."*

And now—this?

Celeste wiped at her cheek, surprised to find a tear there.

She didn't remember starting to cry.

She whispered to the air, more confession than thought: *"What hurts the most is that I don't want her to be guilty. I want me to be wrong."*

But deep down, something darker and quieter murmured back.

You're not wrong.

She stared out at the sandwich shop. Then at the sandwich in her lap.

Still, she couldn't eat.

———

FRIDAY – 4:12 P.M.
LOCATION: CAFÉ VESUVIO, MIDTOWN — A QUIET, NO-FRILLS
SPOT WITH STRONG COFFEE AND WEAKER CELL SERVICE

Celeste arrived early. She always did when she was nervous—a habit formed from years of being the only Black woman in the room and never wanting to give anyone a reason to label her *unprepared.*

The café was nearly empty. A couple of grad students hovered over laptops by the window, and the barista moved slowly, rinsing milk pitchers and humming something from the '90s.

She took a table in the back and ordered a peppermint tea. Her stomach still couldn't handle coffee.

A few minutes later, Kayla walked in—former APEX logistics coordinator, now working for a mid-size competitor across town. She and Celeste hadn't spoken much since the reorg, but Kayla had always been sharp and observant. The kind of person you wanted in a launch meeting. Neutral territory.

"Celeste Monroe, looking like a TED Talk," Kayla teased, sliding into the seat across from her.

Celeste smiled. *"You know me—always giving keynote energy."*

Small talk lasted just long enough for their drinks to arrive. Then Celeste leaned in, keeping her tone light.

"Hey — I wanted to ask you something. Not weird, not official, just... timeline stuff. You remember that Phase 2 vendor contract rollout, right? The one last spring?"

Kayla nodded, curious. *"Yeah, the one where we switched invoicing platforms?"*

"Mmhmm. Do you remember when Valerie came into the loop on that?"

Kayla thought for a moment. *"Pretty early, I think. Like... February? Right after that vendor audit failed. I remember because she told me she had to jump in and 'rescue you from a bad deal.'"*

Celeste blinked. *"Wait — what?"*

Kayla stirred her drink casually. *"Yeah. Not in a shady way. More like, 'I had to jump in and help Celeste out because some stuff slipped through.' I didn't think anything of it."*

Celeste forced a tight smile, nodding as if it made sense. Her insides, however, dropped.

There had been no *"bad deal."*

The audit had flagged a minor discrepancy, one she'd corrected within hours. Valerie hadn't even been directly assigned to that stream yet—at least, not from what Celeste remembered.

But if she'd been telling people   otherwise... If she'd been planting seeds that made Celeste look negligent from the start...

Celeste picked up her tea with a calm hand. *"That's helpful,"* she said smoothly. *"Thanks, Kay."*

"Just tying up loose ends."

Kayla's phone buzzed. *"Ugh, I gotta run—weekly check-in. Let's not wait so long to catch up next time?"*

They hugged briefly, and Kayla disappeared back into the blur of midtown foot traffic.

Celeste remained at the table a few minutes longer, staring into the swirl of her tea, now going cold.

FRIDAY – 8:47 P.M.
LOCATION: CELESTE'S HOME, LIVING ROOM

The house was still.

No music. No television murmuring in the background. Just the soft click of the grandfather clock in the hallway and the occasional creak of the floorboards adjusting to the cool night air.

Celeste sat on the edge of her sofa, barefoot, wrapped in a loose cardigan, the sleeves pulled over her hands like armor.

She lit a single candle—vanilla and sandalwood—and turned off the overhead light. The flicker softened the room, casting golden shadows against the ivory walls.

Her Bible sat in her lap, already opened to *Psalm 27.*

She hadn't picked it randomly. It was a chapter she'd gone to many times before.

"The Lord is my light and my salvation—whom shall I fear?"

She whispered the words aloud. Not for power, not as a declaration—but to *remember.*

To remind her heart that it wasn't alone in the dark. She bowed her head.

"Lord..."

Her voice cracked.

She paused, swallowed, tried again.

"Lord, I don't want to believe what I'm starting to see. I don't want to believe she'd do this. Not Valerie. Not her."

Silence.

She exhaled slowly, staring at the open page. Her thumb traced the verse, then stilled.

"I'm not asking for revenge. I'm not asking You to punish her."

She shook her head. *"I just want the truth. Even if it breaks me. Even if it breaks everything."*

The candle flame trembled slightly, just once.

She sat there for a long time—unmoving, unhurried—until the clock struck nine.

Then, quietly, she closed the Bible, slid it onto the table, and sat back.

No more begging for it *not* to be true.

No more pretending her gut was wrong.

No more flinching at the rising tide.

Celeste Monroe wasn't praying for peace anymore. She was praying for clarity.

And that —That God always gave.

———

The sunlight was barely filtering through the curtains when Celeste rolled over and reached for her phone.

She wasn't expecting anything.

No breaking news. No urgent messages.

Just… another morning.

But there it was.

> **From: Valerie Henshaw**
> **Received: 6:48 a.m.**

> *"Hope you're holding up. Thinking of you."*

No emojis. No exclamation points.

Short. Simple. Carefully measured.

Celeste sat up slowly.

She read it once.

Twice.

A third time.

Her heart didn't race.

Her stomach didn't flip.

There was no pang of warmth, no softening.

Only silence—the kind that comes when your spirit is doing the listening, not your ears.

She held the phone in her hand for a few seconds longer, then opened her messages, took a screenshot, and tapped a name she had memorized now more than most.

To: Atty. Marshall Croft

Attachment: Screenshot

Message: *"I think she knows more than she's letting on."*

Send.

No rage. No heartbreak.

Just the first stone placed on a path she could no longer ignore.

She looked out the window, the sun rising slow and soft behind the clouds.

Last night, she had prayed for truth. Not proof.

Not permission to hate.

Just truth.

And here it was—

A knock on the door of her discernment.

A message not from Valerie, but from **God**:

"I hear you. Now watch Me work."

CHAPTER NINE

NO MORE ILLUSIONS

"Sometimes the person you'd take a bullet for ends up being the one behind the gun."
— Tupac Shakur

MONDAY MORNING

Celeste sat cross-legged at the edge of her guest room bed, laptop balanced on a tray table, a steaming cup of black tea beside her. She had set her alarm early—she wanted the house still, the world quiet, her mind as clear as possible.

Croft's assistant had sent over the first round of discovery materials late Sunday evening—files tied to communications about the disputed contract, especially between APEX senior leadership, Valerie Henshaw, and vendor contacts. Everything Celeste had been shut out of. Everything she was now legally entitled to see.

The file folder was titled:

"Discovery_2023Q4_COMM_vetted.zip."

She unzipped the folder. Her heart was already racing.

She didn't expect to see Valerie's name so many times.

Subject lines blurred past her eyes:

- *FW: Concerns About Celeste Monroe*
- *Re: Project 18T Consolidation – Please Advise*
- *Celeste Feedback – Confidential – Do Not Forward*

She clicked one open. An email from Valerie to Regional Director Lenora Gates, dated over **eighteen months ago**:

> *"Lenora, I hate to bring this to you like this, but I've received some feedback from the vendor team that Celeste's demeanor in meetings is creating confusion. She tends to dominate the conversation and doesn't always clarify ownership. I've cleaned it up where I can, but I just wanted you to be aware. I'm not saying she's unfit — just maybe not ideal for client-facing lead roles right now."*

Celeste's hand went still on the trackpad. Her mouth went dry.

She remembered that time period—it was when she had been under consideration for the Regional Integration Lead role. A huge step up. The same role Valerie said she had *"fought hard"* to get her an interview for. The one she never heard back about.

She opened another email. This one was dated just six weeks before the lawsuit hit.

> *To: Senior Ops Leadership*
> *From: Valerie Henshaw*
>
> *"Just looping back on Monroe's role in the vendor contract timeline — she was involved earlier than she's admitting. I think she's concerned about liability, but I wanted to go on record that I voiced concerns at the time. I don't want any of this to circle back on the department unfairly."*

A breath caught in Celeste's chest.

She hadn't even been in the country when that early contract communication happened. She had receipts. Emails. Travel records.

She blinked hard, re-reading the thread. Valerie hadn't just thrown her under the bus—she'd done it *strategically.*

Another message, this time from over two years ago:

> *"I've coached Celeste through a lot, and I don't think she always understands how her intensity affects morale. I've stepped in when needed, but I can't do it forever."*

And this one:

"If you're considering her for the Q1 Promotion Slate, I'd encourage caution. She's technically strong, yes, but the interpersonal feedback is mixed. Not from me — from others."

Celeste pushed back from the tray table, the laptop still open, and stood up. Her hands were shaking. Her eyes burned.

Three promotions. Three betrayals.

She had believed Valerie. She had trusted her. She'd cried in front of her. Shared scripture with her. Let her pray over her dying mother.

And all that time…

"She was the one behind the gun," Celeste whispered.

Her phone buzzed. A message from Croft:

"Also — review file batch 3B. Some of those threads may require follow-up. We believe these communications are relevant to both your defense and a potential counterclaim."

She stared at the screen. A counterclaim.

Suddenly, the cost of this lawsuit—the $3,000 to $4,000 a week she'd been choking down like bitter medicine—didn't feel like a loss anymore.

It felt like an investment. An investment in the truth.

TUESDAY MORNING

The coffee maker beeped behind her—a small, robotic reminder that life still moved forward. Celeste stood at the kitchen island, cradling her mug in both hands like it might steady her thoughts. She hadn't even taken a sip yet when the notification appeared:

> **Subject:** Croft Legal Services – Weekly Invoice
> **Amount Due:** $3,820.00
> **Due Date:** Net 7 Days

She clicked it open. Itemized. Precise. Cold.

- Email review: $275
- Strategy consult: $600
- Contract analysis: $840
- Paralegal document prep: $485
- Court filing admin: $260
- General counsel (Croft): $1,360

She inhaled slowly. Exhaled slower.

It wasn't that she couldn't pay it—this time. She had savings. Retirement accounts. A few assets she could liquidate if she absolutely had to.

But it was *the burn rate*.

$3,820 this week.
$4,070 last week.
$3,690 the week before that.

It had been twelve weeks of legal hell—and she had already spent over *$36,000.* And they were just entering *discovery.*

She set the mug down and opened her banking app.

Scanned the balances. Did the math in her head. She could cover next week, and the week after that, *maybe* one more after that without pulling from her 401(k).

But after that?

She clicked to her calendar. Five items for the day. Two calls with Croft's team. One meeting with HR. A reschedule notice for her biweekly therapy appointment. And a Friday sit-down to prepare for the next deposition.

The little colored blocks made her stomach turn.

Her job—the one she used to *love*—now felt like a front for the real work: ***fighting for her life.***

She sat at the table, letting the silence wrap around her. A single tear rolled down her cheek, but she didn't wipe it. Didn't flinch.

"You have to pay... to prove you didn't lie. You have to pay to clear your own name."

The thought landed in her chest like a steel weight.

Not one person had ever warned her that justice came with a bill. That *truth* was something you had to mortgage your future for.

And still... she didn't falter.

She closed the invoice. Opened the *"Discovery – Monroe"* folder again. Took another sip of coffee—finally— and pulled her laptop closer.

If Valerie thought this would break her, she didn't know her at all.

Celeste would pay every dollar. She would chase every lie.

TUESDAY AFTERNOON
APEX LOGISTICS

The floor looked the same. Same carpet. Same recycled air. Same half-dead ficus by the elevators. But Celeste could feel it —*something had shifted.*

She stepped off the elevator with her laptop bag over one shoulder and a manila folder tucked against her side. Ahead of her, a team lead she'd worked with on the Harrison rollout turned quickly into the corridor, pretending not to see her.

In the open area near the glass conference rooms, she passed two colleagues huddled near the printer—they quieted mid-sentence as she walked by. Not a malicious silence, but a guarded one. As if they didn't want to be heard. As if *she* wasn't safe to speak around.

Celeste's heels clicked down the hall, too loud in a space that used to feel collaborative, casual. Now, every sound echoed off tension.

She reached the break room. The coffee pot hissed. A microwave beeped.

"...I mean, you can't prove it, but still," someone was whispering, too close to the door. *"She's always been—"*

The moment Celeste stepped in, silence fell like a dropped curtain. One woman offered a tight smile, then immediately busied herself rinsing out a mug. Another man suddenly remembered he left something at his desk and slipped past her, eyes on the floor.

She stood there a moment too long, then poured herself lukewarm coffee, letting the quiet stretch and settle like fog.

She's not guilty — but she's radioactive.

Back in her office, she slid into her chair and opened her inbox. A calendar reminder pinged for a performance review. She barely registered it.

At the door, a junior analyst—Malia, bright and young and two months out of grad school—hesitated before speaking.

"*Celeste?*" she asked quietly.

Celeste turned.

Malia leaned in just slightly. "*Just so you know... not everybody believes what's being said.*"

There was no need to ask what she meant.

Celeste nodded once. "*Thank you.*"

Malia nodded back, and returned to her screen, shoulders tight.

It wasn't betrayal. It was *self-preservation.*

Celeste understood it now. Valerie's toxicity hadn't just bruised her—it had soaked into the fabric of the office. People weren't cruel. They were cautious. Afraid of being caught in Valerie's web. Of making the wrong friend. Saying the wrong thing. Becoming the next scapegoat.

Because deep down, they **knew** something was off. They always had.

"*She's so polished.*"

"*You know Valerie—she can be intense.*"

"I don't know how she does it all, but she always seems to know what's going on..."

It had all been there, in the corners of conversations. They didn't have proof before. But they had instincts.

Celeste could feel it now—this wasn't just a personal betrayal.

It was *systemic rot,* wrapped in scripture quotes and strategic smiles.

And finally, someone was pulling back the curtain.

THURSDAY MORNING – 7:42 AM
VALERIE'S KITCHEN

Valerie's kitchen was quiet, the kind of calm only the early morning could offer. The faint sound of a coffee maker brewing filled the silence as Valerie wiped down the counter, her movements deliberate and precise. She wasn't just cleaning —she was *preparing.*

Her phone buzzed on the countertop, and she reached for it without missing a beat. She'd been sending Celeste check-in messages every few days. The text was always upbeat, always cheerful—always a facade.

"Hope you're hanging in there, Celeste. You've been on my mind. If you need anything, I'm just a call away! – V"

She read it over once more, tapping the emoji with a practiced finger. *Just enough warmth, not too much.*

Satisfied, she hit send and set the phone down beside her coffee mug. Her smile lingered for a second longer than it should have, and she took a sip, staring absently out the window.

Behind her, Marcus walked in, tying his robe. He moved toward the kitchen counter, reaching for a glass of water.

He paused, giving her a look she hadn't quite expected.

"You okay?" His voice was calm, but the concern in it was impossible to miss.

Valerie didn't meet his gaze. She leaned against the counter, smiling wide. *"Of course. Just busy, you know? I've got that huddle this morning. Everyone's on edge."*

She gestured vaguely at her phone. *"It's all about keeping the team motivated, keeping them focused. Everything's fine."*

Marcus eyed her for a beat longer. *"You sleeping okay?"*
Valerie froze for just a moment, then shook her head, forcing another smile. *"Yeah, just... you know, late nights. Lots to manage."*

Her smile didn't quite reach her eyes…it never did.

She felt the pressure of it now—the weight of maintaining this carefully curated version of herself, of being the manager, the friend, the confidante. She'd been doing this for *months*, maybe longer. And it had worked. So far. But lately, the cracks were starting to show, like little fractures she couldn't quite hide.

Marcus, ever the steady presence, gave a small nod but didn't press further. He moved on to grab some eggs, while Valerie turned back to her phone, scrolling absently through her messages. She opened the Zoom app for the team huddle later, ensuring her camera angle was perfect.

"Quick Connect – 10 mins tops"

She had it all under control. At least, that's what she kept telling herself.

As she set the phone down and prepared her mug for another round, Marcus's voice interrupted her thoughts.

"You sure you're alright, Val? You seem a little... off." He hesitated, but his concern was genuine.

Valerie didn't look at him this time, either. She was already moving toward the door. *"I'm fine. Just tired. Nothing to worry about."*

Another lie. A necessary one.

She gathered herself quickly, pushing the discomfort away like a puff of air. It wasn't the first time she'd lied to him, or to herself. But the pressure was different now—Celeste had begun to pull back...and stay there. Things weren't as smooth as they had been. And for the first time, Valerie wasn't sure how long she could keep the illusion going.

As she grabbed a butter croissant and sauntered away, she caught a glimpse of herself in the hallway mirror. The reflection staring back at her was a confident, composed version of herself. But for a split second, something flickered —the image didn't seem to quite match her emotions. The smile was too bright. The eyes too cold.

She had to keep going. She *had* to. Her confidence was her vulnerability. And deep down, she felt it slipping, one moment at a time.

THURSDAY EVENING – 8:15 PM
CELESTE'S LIVING ROOM

The soft hum of her laptop filled the silence in the living room. Celeste had barely eaten, barely moved since her discovery of the last batch of emails. Her mind was overwhelmed, drowning in the details—the lies, the manipulations, the realization that Valerie had known all along how much Celeste had trusted her.

As the phone buzzed on the coffee table, she snapped back to the present. Jason's name lit up the screen. She picked up quickly, a part of her knowing that something was about to shift.

"*Hey,*" she said quietly, leaning back into the couch, rubbing her temples.

"*Hey. You okay?*" Jason's voice was calm but there was something underneath it—something new. He'd been doing the legwork on his end, and it was clear this wasn't just another check-in.

"*I'm getting there,*" Celeste sighed. "*I've been going through more of the files... and it's worse than I thought. Valerie's been covering her tracks so long, I don't even know where to start.*"

Jason was quiet for a moment. When he spoke again, his tone was more focused, more deliberate.

"*I've been thinking about it,*" he started, voice low. "*I've pieced a few things together from what I've seen in the emails, the timelines... it's not just about the lawsuit. It never was.*"

Celeste sat up straighter, her stomach twisting. "*What do you mean?*"

Jason didn't hesitate. "*Valerie needed you in a support role. Not in leadership. You were good at what you did, Celeste—really good. But you made her look good. You kept everything running smoothly, but you were never supposed to move up.*"

Celeste felt a chill go through her. "*What are you saying?*"

"*There was never room for both of you to succeed. The closer you got to a promotion, the more her own weaknesses would have been exposed. And she couldn't afford that. She was already feeling cornered, I think.*"

Celeste's grip on her phone tightened, the realization hitting her like a physical blow. "*So... she kept me in this position, kept me from getting promoted... all for **her** benefit?*"

Jason's voice softened slightly. "*Yeah. She didn't want you to take her position or get higher than her, Celeste. She couldn't risk you stepping into the leadership role she thought was hers. She needed you close enough to control, but not close enough to outshine her.*"

Celeste felt something shift inside her, a sickening feeling twisting her gut. "*She didn't just betray me. She **used** me.*"

Jason paused, his voice quieter now, but with a firmness that Celeste could feel through the line. "*Exactly. She didn't want to lose her asset. You were valuable to her as long as you stayed right where she needed you—in a supporting role, not in the spotlight.*"

The words echoed in Celeste's mind, each one a punch to the chest. It wasn't just about the betrayal. It was about *exploitation*. Valerie hadn't seen Celeste as a colleague, a friend—she'd seen her as a resource, a tool to further her own ambitions. And Celeste had been blind to it all.

The phone felt heavy in Celeste's hand as she processed what Jason had just laid out for her. Her mind flashed back to all the times Valerie had praised her, built her up—only to quietly undermine her at every turn, steering her away from the very thing she'd worked for: recognition, advancement, a chance to lead.

Jason continued, his voice filled with quiet resolve. "*I know this is a lot to take in, but you need to hear it. This wasn't personal, Celeste. It was all about control. Valerie had everything riding on keeping you exactly where you were.*"

She closed her eyes, the weight of the truth settling deep in her chest. *"I can't believe this..."* The words were barely above a whisper, a mix of disbelief and sorrow. *"I never saw it. Not until now."*

Jason's voice was steady, reassuring. *"You don't have to carry this on your own, Celeste. You have me. You have us. And we're not going to stop until we get this right."*

Celeste nodded, even though he couldn't see her. It was a small comfort, but it helped ground her. *"Thanks, Jason. I—I needed to hear that. I just..."* She paused, letting out a long breath. *"It's hard. I thought I knew her. I thought we had something real."*

"You did," Jason said firmly. *"But she was playing a different game, Celeste. And now it's your turn."*

Celeste glanced at the emails once more—the damning proof of Valerie's sabotage, the lies about her personality, the backhanded comments that had blocked her from the opportunities she deserved. *All of it was real. All of it was Valerie.*

And now, Celeste was ready to stop playing by Valerie's rules. *"Alright,"* Celeste said, her voice steady but with a new edge of determination. *"Let's take her down."*

Celeste sat at her desk, the glow of her laptop screen illuminating the darkness of the room. The emails were open in front of her—every email, every message, every detail of Valerie's manipulation. The truth was all there, staring back at her, and she knew this was the final moment. There would be no more running from it.

She didn't feel anger or rage. No tears. No screams. Her emotions were too deep, too quiet for that. Instead, she felt a cold determination settle in her chest.

The emails from Valerie, the ones that had once felt like confirmation of a partnership, a friendship—they were nothing but lies, carefully constructed to trap Celeste in a web of deceit. Now, each one was a cold, calculated move in Valerie's game, and Celeste was finally ready to face it.

With steady hands, Celeste clicked through the emails, one by one, saving them all to her hard drive. The weight of the task settled over her like a heavy cloak, but it was the only way forward. She created a new folder, the words *"Truth, in her own words"* flashing across the screen as she typed them out. She stared at the name for a moment, as though it was a warning. A promise.

When the last file was saved, Celeste closed her laptop with a soft click. The room felt still and silent around her, the weight of what had just happened sinking in. There was no turning back now. The truth had been unearthed.

She set the laptop down on the table, her hand lingering on it for a moment longer than necessary. She could feel the tension in her body, but it didn't crack. She wouldn't let it.

Taking a slow breath, Celeste whispered the words, barely audible but heavy with meaning:

"God, give me the strength to finish this."

The weight of the moment hung in the air, and for the first time in a long time, Celeste felt a sense of peace, quiet but undeniable. The truth was out. And now, she would fight to make sure it was seen.

––––––––––

CHAPTER TEN

THE COST OF KNOWING

*"Wisdom is the principal thing; therefore get wisdom: and
with all thy getting get understanding."*
— *Proverbs 4:7 (KJV)*

The hum of the refrigerator was the only sound in the room.
Celeste sat alone at her kitchen table, a half-empty mug of cold
tea beside her, forgotten. The overhead light cast a harsh glow
across the stack of paper in front of her—invoices,
spreadsheets, envelopes, and receipts. The numbers blurred
slightly on the page, but she didn't blink them away. She knew
what they said. Knew too well what they meant.

$204,378.19.

That was the total as of today.

She'd written it in black ink at the bottom of a legal pad,
circling it three times—each pass darker, heavier than the last.

The page beneath it was dented from the pressure. That number represented nearly everything she'd saved over the last decade. Gone. Not stolen. Not misplaced. Spent.

Celeste pressed the pad of her thumb into the bridge of her nose and exhaled slowly. Her temples ached, not from lack of sleep —she hadn't slept well in months—but from the pressure that never left her. This was supposed to be the stage of life where she was building something—not defending it all from ruin.

A soft rustle broke the silence. She looked up and saw her cat, Sable, weaving between the table legs before leaping effortlessly onto the counter. Celeste raised an eyebrow.

"You're not supposed to be up there," she said gently, her voice hoarse from disuse.

Sable blinked slowly at her, utterly unfazed, and stretched out with the lazy entitlement of a creature untouched by litigation. Celeste stared at her, almost envious.

She reached across the table and brushed a curled corner of a forensics report flat with her fingertips. The name of the technical firm was printed at the top—a company she hadn't even heard of a year ago, but who had billed her nearly twenty thousand dollars to trace document metadata, server access logs, and digital correspondence chains. All of it necessary. All of it leading toward the truth.

And still, it wasn't enough.

The legal case had passed the two-year mark. Discovery had ended months ago, but delays, continuances, and a revolving door of uncooperative witnesses had kept the case in purgatory. Valerie—calculating, quiet, careful Valerie—had covered her tracks well. Not perfectly, but well enough to stall resolution. And that was the game she played: delay, deny, disappear.

Celeste leaned back and let her head rest against the high wooden chair. Her eyes flicked to the ceiling, blinking away the burn of tears that wouldn't fall. She hadn't cried in a long time. Not because she wasn't overwhelmed—she was. Every single day. But because crying felt like a luxury she couldn't afford. Not when there was still a chance to make this right. Not when there were still people—like Damien—who deserved her fight.

She turned her gaze toward the window. The night beyond the glass was black, her own reflection faintly staring back at her —tired eyes, hollow cheeks, resolve carved into every line of her face.

"I didn't ask for this," she whispered. *"But I won't let her win."* She meant it.

Her phone buzzed softly. A notification. She didn't even glance at it. The world outside this war—texts, Instagrams, dinner invitations she no longer received—felt distant. Unreal.

She reached across the table again, this time grabbing a folder labeled *"Valerie – Internal Comms (2019)"*, and slid it closer. Another stack to review. More dots to connect. Valerie thought she was safe. Thought she could spin lies and hide behind performance and proximity. But Celeste had seen enough now to understand the playbook.

The betrayal wasn't just personal. It was surgically engineered.

Sable meowed softly, then curled herself into a tight circle on the granite. Celeste glanced at her and managed a faint smile. Her one unchanging constant. No lies. No manipulation. Just quiet loyalty.

Celeste's smile faded as her eyes returned to the documents.

"*I'll finish this*," she said, this time louder—to herself, to the empty house, to the God who had watched it all unfold. "*No matter what it costs.*"
The weight in her chest didn't ease, but it steadied. There was power in the decision. Not just to endure, but to outlast.

She rose from the table, stretched the stiffness from her limbs, and walked toward the hallway. At the last second, she paused, turned back, and gathered the invoices into a single neat stack.

She carried them to her home office and slipped them into a drawer. Out of sight for now. But not forgotten.

The fight wasn't over. But neither was she.

The blinds were angled just so, letting in the perfect stream of sunlight across Valerie's desk—not too harsh, not too dim. Her coffee sat beside her in a sleek travel mug with "#BOSS" in bold rose gold, steam long gone but untouched. She hadn't taken a sip in over an hour. The ritual mattered more than the drink itself.

She tapped through a spreadsheet with perfectly manicured nails, her face impassive, a study in corporate composure. No one would guess her internal monologue was a loop of shallow affirmations: *Everything is fine. Stay calm. It's almost over.*

A soft knock at the door broke her rhythm. Without looking up, she called, *"Come in."*

It was one of the junior analysts—Anthony—standing stiffly with a document in hand.

"Just need your signature on the budget projection, Valerie."

She smiled, warm and efficient. *"Of course, Anthony. Leave it there, I'll sign it in a bit."*

He nodded and left as quickly as he came. Valerie watched the door close, her smile fading just slightly. She used to love her reputation—calm, composed, competent. For years now people's energy was off. Skittish. Careful. She chalked it up to the lawsuit drama. That kind of scandal made people nervous. Understandably.

She glanced at her phone. No new texts from Celeste, not that she expected any. Celeste had gone completely quiet and almost fully remote. Probably broke. Probably exhausted. Probably ready to cave and settle, just like Valerie had predicted. If Celeste had any sense, she'd be looking for a graceful way out.

Valerie opened her Messages app anyway and scrolled through their old threads. One in particular from three years ago caught her eye—a photo of a cake Celeste had baked after a big team win. Valerie had captioned it: *Powerhouse duo. You and me.*

She smirked, amused at her own performance. How easy it had been to build trust. How natural it had seemed to pull the strings while Celeste took the stage.

"*Some people just aren't built for leadership,*" Valerie muttered under her breath.

Her phone buzzed—a text from her husband.

> **Nathan:** "*How's your day so far? You sounded stressed earlier.*"

Valerie rolled her eyes and sighed. *Of course I sounded stressed,* she thought. *I'm two years behind on my early retirement because Celeste Monroe refuses to lie down and disappear.*

She tapped back a response, fingers flying.

> **Valerie:** "*Just the usual. Work drama, too many meetings. It'll all smooth out soon.*"

She hesitated, then added:

Valerie: *"I promise I'm okay."*

It wasn't a complete lie. Not in her mind. She *was* okay. Or at least, she *would* be once this whole ridiculous case finally closed and she could cash in on her carefully built exit strategy. Sure, the deal she'd planned—quiet stock reallocations, a well-timed company pivot, and her name conveniently cleared of blame—had been pushed back indefinitely. But nothing was ruined. Just... delayed.

The delays were Celeste's fault, anyway. Always digging. Always reacting. Valerie had figured the pressure would break her months ago. But if the stress didn't snap her, the money drain surely would. Valerie knew how much legal fees cost, especially for that top tier firm she was working with. She'd done the math. No one could keep that kind of fight going for long.

Valerie clicked open her browser and checked the court docket again—something she did every few days, not because she expected anything, but just in case. Today's update was mundane: a continuance filed by the opposing counsel, motion deadline extended. She exhaled with a little smirk.

More delays. More proof that this thing is limping to an end.

She leaned back in her chair and glanced at the vision board she'd hung beside her desk. It was full of glossy magazine clippings: a lake house, a white kitchen with gold fixtures, the phrase *"Financial Freedom at 50"* in bold letters. The board had been her birthday gift to herself a few years ago, the same year the plan was put into motion. The same year she had quietly sabotaged her own team to make Celeste the fall person.

Everything would have worked—if Celeste had just accepted the blame.

She turned back to her screen and began replying to emails, putting on the same polished, helpful tone she always used.

No one suspected her.

Well—*maybe* Jason had sensed something. He'd mentioned once or twice that she was *"very different lately."* But men didn't want to dig. Not really. They wanted to be reassured. And Valerie had become excellent at giving just enough truth to keep his questions soft.

The only person who ever *really* saw her, saw all of her, had been Celeste. That was what made this so... poetic. Celeste had trusted her. Had leaned on her. Had followed her guidance like a disciple. And now? Valerie smiled to herself.

Now she's burning through her savings and her sanity trying to prove a lie no one will believe.

She didn't see the storm forming behind her. Didn't know just how many documents Celeste's legal team had uncovered. Didn't understand that every delay, every postponed hearing, was buying Celeste more time. More leverage. More truth.

Valerie believed she was still in control. And that belief, more than anything else, was her blind spot.

The overhead light buzzed softly, casting a cold glow over the files spread across Celeste's desk. Outside her office window, the city was swallowed in twilight, the buildings across the way turning into gray silhouettes against the deepening sky. She hadn't eaten dinner. Again. There was no point. Her stomach clenched at the sight of the ever-growing stack of legal correspondence and billing summaries.

Her phone buzzed—*Croft, Esq.* lit up on the screen.

She answered on the first ring. *"Evening, Croft."*

"Celeste," his tone was steady, but weary. *"Got a few updates for you."*

She sat back in her chair, shoulders already braced for disappointment.

"First," he continued, *"you're not going to love this. The deposition for the IT subcontractor from Q3? Postponed. His attorney filed a protective order — claims his testimony would violate confidentiality agreements."*

Celeste closed her eyes briefly. *"So that's what… the third key witness this month that's dodged us?"*

"Fourth," Croft corrected, *"if you count the internal auditor who suddenly took an indefinite leave of absence."*

Of course. Another delay. Another ghost in the machine.

"But," he added quickly, *"there's progress. The forensic audit team traced a few irregular payment structures. We're seeing financial patterns that don't match Valerie's salary grade— discretionary bonuses signed off through an old vendor contract you flagged years ago. It's obscure, but they're digging."*

Celeste stared at the framed photo of her mother on the bookshelf—the one taken at her church's Easter brunch years ago. Her mother's smile had always been her anchor. Now it just hurt to look at.

"She covered her tracks well," Celeste murmured.

"She did," Croft agreed. *"But not perfectly. These things take time. Think of it as erosion, not explosion. We're wearing it down."*

Celeste sighed. Her voice, when it came, was quiet. *"I don't even know who I am outside this fight anymore."*

"You're someone still standing," Croft said gently. *"And that's more than most could say."*

She hung up a few minutes later, but didn't move. Her fingers curled into a fist in her lap.

Two years.

Over two hundred thousand dollars.

And still, Valerie had her life. Her job. Her reputation.

———————

The house was quiet, save for the soft hum of the dishwasher cycling in the kitchen. Valerie sat on the edge of her bed, legs crossed neatly, brushing a lock of hair behind her ear as she updated the spreadsheet she kept hidden deep in a password-protected folder on her laptop. A column labeled *Contingency Fund* stared back at her—a dwindling balance paired with projections she'd massaged one too many times to still call realistic.

Across the room Nathan shuffled toward the bathroom. Valerie clicked the laptop closed.

He came back a few minutes later, toweling his face. *"You still working?"*

"Just wrapping up. Things are busy," she replied, the practiced cadence of calm in her voice. *"Everything's moving forward. Just a few more weeks."*

Nathan sat beside her. His eyes were soft, tired. *"You've been saying that for months."*

She smiled, tight-lipped. *"That's how business is. You know that."*

He reached for her hand. *"I'm proud of you. I know it's been tough. But you're keeping it together."*

Valerie nodded, eyes watering slightly—not from emotion, but fatigue. Or maybe both. *"God's been faithful."*

They knelt beside the bed, their routine intact even if everything else felt held together by threads. Valerie laced her fingers through Nathan's and began to pray.

"Lord, you know the stress we've carried. You know the battles I'm facing. Help me stand strong. Let no weapon formed against me prosper. Let justice prevail, and Your will be done. In Jesus' name, amen."

Nathan added a soft amen, and kissed her forehead before pulling back the covers.

Valerie stayed kneeling longer than usual, staring at the carpet. The house was too still.

Her plan should have worked by now.

Celeste was supposed to crack under the pressure. Resign. Settle. Disappear. Not drag this out for two years.

Valerie stood, moving to the window, looking out into the darkened street. Somewhere out there, Celeste was still fighting —and still standing.

No matter. The delays were blessings in disguise. God's timing, not hers.

That's what she told herself.

––––––––––

Celeste sat in her dining room, laptop propped open, the soft clink of her cat's paws padding around in the background. A candle flickered beside her, not for ambiance—just to remind her something still burned that wasn't rage.

The Zoom screen blinked to life. Croft's square appeared first, followed by Amelia (their firm's associate), then Greg from the forensics team, and finally the ever-tense paralegal, Jodie, typing before her video even connected.

"*Okay,*" Croft started, pulling everyone into focus. "*We need to talk strategy for pre-trial. The court's logjammed. The judge is backlogged by at least six weeks. We're looking at early fall, best case.*"

Celeste let out a slow breath. "*Of course.*"

Amelia chimed in. "*Witness cooperation is still spotty. No-shows. Cancellations. It's giving the other side more time to posture.*"

"*But,*" Greg said, tapping something on his screen, "*we're tracking down a shell account we believe Valerie used to authorize discretionary funds from the joint training budget. If that holds, it proves she rerouted money to inflate her team's performance."*

Celeste leaned forward. *"That was Damien's territory. She used me to frame him—and the bonus funds helped her team meet metrics that quarter. She built the whole 'promotion' on it."*

"We think so," Greg nodded.

Silence hung for a moment, thick and charged.

Then Celeste said it. *"I want to add a counterclaim."*

Croft looked up. *"For?"*

"Malicious interference. Emotional damages. Maybe even defamation. She manipulated me into a role that was designed to explode, and now I've spent two years clawing my way out."

Amelia tilted her head. *"It's bold. Valid. But risky. The judge doesn't like extra filings unless there's airtight evidence."*

"He'll call it noise," Croft added. *"Might even threaten to sever the claims or delay the main hearing. You sure?"*

Celeste glanced toward the hallway. Her cat sat there, blinking slowly, tail curled neatly around her feet. Watching her. Still. Faithful.

"I'm sure," she said.

Croft nodded slowly. *"Then we'll prepare it. We've come this far. Might as well say the whole truth when we finally speak."*

For the first time that day, Celeste felt something other than exhaustion. It wasn't relief, not yet. But it was purpose.

She was going to make sure the court heard everything. Even if it meant losing more time. Even if it meant risking more of herself.

It was nearly midnight, but Valerie lay wide-eyed beneath the duvet, staring at the shadows on the ceiling. Nathan was already asleep, his breathing slow and even. The silence pressed in like a weight.

She turned and reached for her phone again.

Unlocked it.

Checked her work email.

Nothing urgent.

But one message from a colleague caught her eye—short, cold, dismissive.

"Thanks. We'll revisit."

No smiley. No warmth. Odd.

She opened her calendar. A meeting she had been leading for months was abruptly canceled by the director. No reschedule. No reason.

She frowned. Her heart beat a little faster.

She opened a browser window and typed her name.

Still nothing. No news stories. No internal memos leaked online. No LinkedIn whispers.

But something felt... off. Like a cold wind under the door.

She tossed the phone on the nightstand, then snatched it back up, her fingers moving quickly.

> **Text to Pastor Melvin**:
> *"Please pray for my peace. I'm under spiritual attack again."*

She stared at the message for a second before hitting send. The phone buzzed back almost immediately:

> **Pastor Melvin**:
> *"Lifting you up now, sister. The enemy attacks hardest before your breakthrough. Stand firm."*

Valerie closed her eyes, clinging to the words like armor. *Stand firm. Breakthrough.*

But even prayer couldn't quiet the buzz in her chest, the tightness around her ribs.

Somewhere, something was moving against her.

She just couldn't see it yet.

———————

CHAPTER ELEVEN

COLLATERAL DAMAGE

"The arc of the moral universe is long, but it bends toward justice."
— Martin Luther King Jr.

The walls of Croft's office were lined with neat rows of law books, thick spines in shades of mahogany and navy, all screaming order and logic in a world where Celeste had experienced nothing but chaos. She sat at the long walnut conference table, her hands wrapped around a mug of untouched herbal tea. Outside the window, the city was still waking, but inside the room, it felt like the day had already been won or lost.

Celeste had lost weight—noticeable now in the sharpness of her collarbones and the way her blazer didn't quite hug her shoulders anymore. Her once-easy smile had hardened over the last two and a half years, replaced by a quiet, focused gaze that cut through pleasantries.

Croft slid the counterclaim packet across the table toward her. *"It's ready,"* he said simply.

Dana, his junior associate, sat to his left. Younger, a bit softer in approach, but whip-smart. *"Before you sign, just know—the judge could see this as retaliatory,"* she warned gently, her tone not dismissive, just honest.

Celeste didn't flinch. *"It's not retaliation,"* she said, her voice clear, low, and unwavering. *"It's restitution."*

The weight of that word hung in the air.

Croft gave a slow nod, his expression unreadable, but the corners of his mouth lifted—just barely.

On the laptop in front of them, Jason's face filled the screen. He was in his truck, parked on a dusty lot near one of his construction sites, wearing a hard hat with his name printed across the front in permanent marker. The sound of machinery buzzed faintly in the background, but his focus was entirely on her.

"I stepped away for this," he said, his eyes earnest. *"Because this matters. You have every right, Cel. You don't owe Valerie your silence—not after everything. Not after Damien."*

The name landed in the room like a dropped glass. Celeste blinked once, slowly. Her jaw tightened, but she didn't look away.

Damien.

His name still carried weight. The first real casualty in Valerie's campaign of destruction. The man whose reputation had been shredded in the same way Valerie had tried to destroy hers. Celeste had seen what the weight of false accusation did to a person. She had lived it. Was still living it.

Croft turned the final page toward her, pen clipped neatly to the top corner.

Intentional Infliction of Emotional Distress.

Fraud.

Malicious Prosecution.

Each word was a monument to the suffering Celeste had endured—and a warning to Valerie that her games were no longer unchecked.

Celeste picked up the pen and signed, her hand steady.

Jason exhaled softly through the speaker. "Let her   feel uncomfortable for a change," he said.

Celeste glanced at the paperwork once more, then set the pen down with finality. *"She doesn't get to rewrite this story,"* she said. *"Not anymore."*

For the first time in months, she felt a shift—small, almost imperceptible, but real. A sense that maybe this wasn't just survival anymore.

It was reclamation.

Valerie sat at her polished mahogany desk, adjusting the hem of her blouse and mentally reviewing the notes for the department meeting. She was too focused on her own preparations to notice the subtle shift in the air—the way the hallway outside her office had quieted, or the fact that a few coworkers had gone strangely silent as they passed by. It wasn't until the knock came that she looked up, snapping out of her autopilot routine.

A man stood in the doorway. Tall, in a suit that screamed professionalism, but his eyes were guarded—almost pitying. He held an envelope in one hand.

"*Valerie Henshaw?*" His voice was curt, but with a hint of something almost sympathetic.

Valerie blinked. "*Yes?*" She straightened in her chair, instinctively smoothing her skirt, her eyes narrowing. Was it a delivery? Some kind of office paperwork?

He stepped closer, not waiting for an invitation. "*You've been served,*" he said, the words landing between them with a finality that seemed too loud for such a quiet room.

Her heart tripped in her chest. The words felt like a blow, a sharp jab. "*Served?*" she echoed, confusion clouding her thoughts. The envelope seemed too thick, too official. Her hand instinctively recoiled, but the process server pushed it toward her, as if it had to happen.

Her fingers brushed the paper, clammy with nervous sweat, and she took the envelope, too quickly, too stiffly. He didn't wait for a thank you or even a response, already turning away, his business done. The faint click of his shoes receded down the hall, and Valerie was left alone, the weight of the envelope heavier than any she'd ever held.

She stared at it for a moment, a strange panic rising in her chest. This wasn't a social call. The unsettling, anonymous nature of it gnawed at her. She knew, without even needing to open it, that this wasn't just paperwork—this was personal. Very personal.

The office felt suddenly too small, too hot. Valerie's palms were slick as she slid the envelope open, her hands shaking slightly as she retrieved the contents. The paper inside was crisp, formal—and all too familiar. She flicked through it with an increasing sense of dread, her stomach sinking with each page.

The counterclaim was there, bold in its accusation. And there, at the very top, her own name. Valerie Henshaw.

Her breath caught in her throat. She wasn't a witness anymore. She wasn't an observer in this entire mess. She was the defendant.

It was as if the world had momentarily stopped spinning, and all that remained was the paper in her hand. Her head swam.

She read the claim again, slower this time. *Intentional Infliction of Emotional Distress. Fraud. Malicious Prosecution.*

"*This can't be happening*," she whispered, her voice trembling, breath shallow.

The office around her blurred. Her vision wavered as the truth of it sank in: this wasn't just about a ruined reputation anymore. This was about her. About everything she'd worked for—the lie she'd lived, the secret she'd kept, the smooth facade that she had restlessly labored to maintain was now on the brink of a dramatic collapse.

Her pulse drummed in her ears, and she felt hot, then cold. Panic threatened to swallow her whole.

With trembling fingers, she pulled her phone from her purse, her movements mechanical. She didn't want to think, didn't want to feel the crushing weight of the accusation. She typed a message to Nathan, her husband—the only person she could pretend was in her corner, even if he had no idea what was really happening.

"*Rough day. Can we talk tonight?*"

She stared at the screen, waiting for the response, her hands too unsteady to hold the phone properly.

Seconds later, the ping of a reply flashed on the screen.

"*Long day here too. Madison has piano. Let's catch up later.*"

Valerie read the message again, the words searing into her chest. Of course. Madison had piano. Nathan had his work, his distractions. The world was moving on around her, while she stood frozen in her office, a defendant now, tangled in a net of her own making.

Her breath came in short bursts, and for a moment, she couldn't move. She closed her eyes, trying to gather herself, but it was no use. This wasn't the clean, simple ending she'd envisioned. This was messy. This was real.

She slammed the phone onto the desk and reached for the envelope again, re-reading the documents, her eyes frantic, scanning for some loophole, some out—anything to deny the words in front of her. But there was nothing. No escape. She couldn't outrun it anymore.

She closed the door to her office, the click of the latch sounding too final in the silence.

Sitting back in her chair, her fingers curled into the armrests, Valerie felt a cold sweat prickling at her skin. She didn't know how much longer she could keep pretending she had control. She had always been able to manage, to spin things in her favor, to talk her way out of trouble. But now? Now, the walls were closing in.

This can't be happening. She couldn't shake the thought. But the truth—the crushing, undeniable truth—was staring her in the face. This wasn't just about her losing a case. This was about everything unraveling.

And there was no way to stop it.

———

The fluorescent lights overhead hummed in the quiet office as Celeste sat at the polished wood conference table, a pile of documents in front of her. The weight of the papers—emails, financial records, testimony transcripts—seemed to press on her chest, suffocating her. She couldn't look away from the binder in front of her, even though her eyes were starting to blur. Every document, every piece of evidence, was a reminder of what Valerie had done, what she had cost Celeste.

Croft, who had been her attorney for nearly three years now, leaned over a set of papers, his eyes narrowed in thought. His sharp features were set in concentration, but Celeste could tell by the way his hands trembled slightly that this was personal for him too.

"She'll deflect," Croft said, his voice low but confident. *"She'll act like she doesn't remember. She'll deny everything, even the things we know she's done. But we have the receipts. We have the proof. We have everything she can't wiggle out of."*

Celeste's fingers gripped the edge of the table, her knuckles turning white. She hadn't let herself think about the deposition too much—she'd been too focused on keeping her head above water. But now, as Croft laid out the strategy, she felt a cold rush of determination.

Dana, the younger associate with dark, sleek hair and a sharp eye, flipped through the binder with methodical precision. *"We have email patterns,"* she said, tapping a section in the binder. *"Expense reports, inconsistent testimony from prior depositions. She's lied under oath before, and we can prove it."*

Celeste barely reacted. The flood of evidence had been overwhelming for months, and it wasn't like the truth could be any more obvious. The deeper they dug into Valerie's finances, the more damning the discovery. Valerie's world was coming undone, piece by piece, but Celeste knew it wasn't going to be easy. Valerie had played dirty, and the woman was nothing if not crafty.

The door clicked open, and Jason stepped in, his presence a familiar comfort. He was a few minutes early, but Celeste appreciated the small gesture. He hadn't been involved in the case for a while, but today, his name was listed as a supplemental witness, someone who could testify to Valerie's retaliation.

He didn't waste time with pleasantries. *"I've got a statement for you guys,"* he said, holding up a manila envelope. *"Figured it might help you with the deposition prep."*

He tossed the envelope onto the table, and Dana immediately opened it. Jason took a seat next to Celeste, leaning back slightly, his fingers tapping lightly against the chair arm.

"She called me a 'risk,'" Jason continued, his voice low but steady. *"Said I was too close to Celeste. Like my loyalty to her*

was a liability." He paused, looking at Croft and Dana. "*That's retaliation, right?*"

Dana didn't hesitate. "*Exactly. And it strengthens our case.*"

Jason's face was calm, but Celeste could see the frustration simmering beneath the surface. Valerie had always been a calculating woman, but to hear it laid out like this—the way she'd treated Jason, as if his loyalty was something to be dismissed—it made Celeste's blood boil. Jason had been nothing but supportive throughout this entire ordeal, and Valerie had slapped him down without a second thought.

Celeste's chest tightened. *This was her line in the sand.* They weren't just defending themselves anymore. They were going on the offense, striking at Valerie's reputation, her lies, her deception. They were calling her out in ways that Celeste hadn't dared to imagine.

Croft sat back in his chair, his hands steepled in front of him. His eyes met Celeste's with a steady gaze. "*This is your line in the sand,*" he said, his voice serious, cutting through the noise. "*You're doing what most people would never dare to. You're taking the fight to her. You're showing the world who she really is.*"

Celeste held his gaze. The weight of his words settled on her chest like an anchor, but there was something else beneath the surface—a sense of power, of control. For the first time in two years, it felt like she was no longer just reacting. She wasn't merely a victim anymore. She was an active participant in this battle, and she was ready to wield the truth like a weapon.

The exhaustion was still there, gnawing at her, but something inside of her had shifted. She had nothing left to lose, and that realization filled her with a dark sense of clarity. Her world had already been shattered, and now, she was rebuilding it, piece by piece, by tearing Valerie down.

"*I'm ready,*" she said, her voice calm, but edged with a strength she hadn't known she possessed. "*I'll do whatever it takes.*"

Croft nodded. "*We'll make sure you're prepared. You know the facts. Stick to the facts.*"

Celeste nodded, her fingers curling around the edge of the table once more. The words in front of her weren't just pages of legal jargon—they were her life, her story, her truth. And now, with every new piece of evidence they uncovered, with every new blow they landed on Valerie's carefully constructed empire, Celeste could feel herself growing stronger.

"*This is it,*" she said, her voice low, almost a whisper. "*This is how we end it.*"

There was a moment of silence in the room as everyone let that sink in. The stakes were higher now. They weren't just after justice. They were after something deeper, something more personal.

The battle wasn't over, but Celeste could see the finish line ahead. She had no idea what it would cost her to get there, but there was no turning back. Not now. Not when she was this close.

The kitchen lights cast a soft glow on the marble countertops, the kind that should've felt calming, but instead, everything felt off. Valerie sat at the kitchen table, papers scattered around her like a chaotic map to her downfall. She had avoided this moment all day, the moment when she had to face the consequences of everything she had done, everything she had covered up. But there was no escaping it now. The counterclaim had shattered her confidence, exposed her for the liar she was.

Nathan, always the calm in their home, moved around the kitchen with his usual ease, pouring two glasses of wine. The soft clink of the glass echoed in the quiet room, too loud for Valerie's fraying nerves.

"You've been quiet all night," Nathan said, his voice gentle but probing.

Valerie didn't lift her head from the papers, pretending to focus on the document in front of her. She couldn't meet his eyes. Not now. Not when she was this close to losing everything.

"Just tired," Valerie muttered, her voice barely more than a whisper.

Nathan set the wineglass in front of her, his gaze lingering for a moment longer than usual. *"Is this about work?"* he asked, his tone careful, as though he already knew the answer but was testing the waters.

Valerie scoffed, picking up the glass without looking at him. *"It's always about work,"* she snapped. Her words were sharp, defensive, but she couldn't bring herself to soften them. Not tonight.

Nathan didn't push. He never did. He didn't know the full extent of what was happening, but he could tell something was wrong. Valerie had always kept her secrets, but now, they were beginning to spill out—crater sized cracks in her carefully crafted facade, visible to anyone who cared to look.

She took a long sip of the wine, the tartness hitting her tongue, but it didn't ease the tension gnawing at her insides. Her heart was racing, a dull thud in her chest that wouldn't quiet.

Madison's voice drifted in from the next room, a soft hum as she read on the sofa. The innocence of it—the quiet simplicity of her daughter's world—was almost too much to bear. Valerie had protected that world. She had built that world. But now, it was all slipping away. All of it.

Nathan sat across from her, swirling his wine in the glass, watching her through the dim light.

"You sure you're okay?" he asked, voice gentle.

There was concern in his eyes, but Valerie could feel the distance in his tone too. He was worried, but he didn't know how deep the hole had become.

Valerie put the glass down with a soft clink, swallowing the lump in her throat. *"I'm fiiiine,"* she lied, her words flat and lifeless.

Nathan didn't respond. He just looked at her for a long moment, his eyes searching for something. Valerie wanted to scream at him to stop looking at her like that, to stop seeing through the cracks she had so carefully hidden. But instead, she picked up the papers again, pretending to be absorbed by the mess in front of her, as though if she focused hard enough, it would all disappear.

Eventually, he sighed and stood up.

"I'm going to check on Madison," he said, his voice softer now, more resigned.

Valerie nodded absently, not looking up from the papers. She heard his footsteps fade into the distance, and the sound of Madison's gentle humming filled the silence that followed.

The moment she was alone, Valerie's body seemed to collapse inward. She pushed the papers away, unable to stand the weight of them for one more second. She stood up and made her way to the bathroom, locking the door behind her with a shaky hand.

The mirror reflected back a woman she didn't recognize. The makeup she had spent so much time perfecting was smudged, streaked down her face like a mask falling away. She barely recognized the woman staring back at her—her eyes tired, her skin pale and taut, her jaw tight with the effort to keep it together.

In the dim light of the bathroom, Valerie's breath came out in shallow, controlled bursts. She stood there for a long moment, staring at her reflection, the words she had been whispering to herself all evening repeating in her head like a mantra.

"*She won't win,*" Valerie whispered to the mirror, her voice shaking despite her effort to sound certain. "*She can't win.*"

But as she said the words, they lost their conviction. There was no more belief in her voice. She knew, deep down, that Celeste wasn't going to back down. The counterclaim, the subpoenas, the mounting evidence—it was too much. Valerie had always counted on her ability to control the situation, to manipulate the narrative, but now, everything was falling out of her grasp. The truth was closing in, and she couldn't control it. She couldn't stop it.

Her mascara had long since run, streaking dark lines down her face. She wiped at it furiously, as though trying to erase the reality staring back at her. The woman in the mirror didn't look like the Valerie Henshaw she had built—the successful, untouchable woman with a plan. This woman looked worn, broken, and scared.

A shudder wracked her body. *What is happening to me?*

She let out a breath that felt more like a sob, but she swallowed it quickly. *No. She wouldn't cry. Not now.*

But her resolve was fraying at the edges, and she could feel it. She wasn't ready for the consequences of her actions. She had never thought about them—never imagined that one day, her lies would turn against her so completely. She'd always thought she could wiggle free, make it all go away. But this was different. Celeste had dug in her heels, and now Valerie was feeling the full weight of her betrayal.

The door to the bathroom creaked slightly as Nathan called softly from the hallway, his voice a gentle reminder of the life she was about to lose.

"You okay in there?"

Valerie took a deep breath, wiped her face, and glanced back at the woman in the mirror. She wasn't ready to face Nathan—not yet.

"I'm fine," she called back, her voice betraying her, trembling in ways she couldn't hide. *"Just give me a minute."*

She heard him sigh, but he didn't push.

Valerie closed her eyes for a brief moment, willing herself to find the strength to stand tall again. She couldn't let this crack widen. She couldn't let Nathan see what was really happening to her.

But deep down, she knew: this was only the beginning of the end.

The house was still, cloaked in the quiet hum of midnight. The shadows of the tall windows stretched across the polished hardwood floors, and the only sound came from the low purring of Sable, curled contentedly at the foot of the couch.

Celeste sat in the corner of the sectional, knees pulled up beneath an old throw blanket, the soft glow of her laptop screen the only light in the room. She should have been sleeping. Her body begged for it. But rest had become a stranger—something that teased her in moments of quiet before slipping away again.

The house—3,200 square feet of curated calm inside a gated community—felt cavernous at night, as if it echoed the voids in her spirit. The space that had once been a symbol of achievement, peace, independence, now felt too large for just her. Too hollow.

A faint chime broke the silence.

Ping.

She looked down. New email.

> **Subject:** Subpoena Return - Henshaw/HR Emails
> **Sender:** Dana Roswell

Celeste's pulse ticked up slightly, though she didn't know why. Most of what came through discovery was uneventful—

deposition confirmations, dull transcripts, expense logs. But Dana didn't email at midnight unless it was something big.

She clicked.

Dana had written only a single line:

"Thought you should see this before morning."

Below was a forwarded string of internal emails between Valerie and the HR Director—dated two weeks *before* Valerie filed her initial complaint.

Celeste's eyes scanned quickly, her breath catching as the cursor hovered over the forwarded content.

> **From:** Valerie Henshaw
> **To:** Lisa Ayers (HR)
> **Date:** March 8, 2023
> **Subject:** Preliminary Concerns – Monroe

"We need to document everything going forward. If this escalates, I want a trail. We'll frame it like Celeste was disruptive—volatile under pressure. Get ahead of her. You know how she gets when she's pushed."

"I'll loop in Malcolm for cover, but let's be smart about this. This won't just protect me—it protects the department. We don't need another Hope situation."

Celeste blinked, rereading the message as though her eyes had betrayed her. *Frame it like Celeste was disruptive. Get ahead of her.*

Her stomach twisted.

The language was surgical. Cold. Intentional.

Premeditated.

She leaned back slowly, the blanket slipping from her shoulders as the reality of the document settled over her like dust. She felt the sharp chill of betrayal again, but not the kind that pierced with fresh pain. This was the steady ache of validation—a confirmation of what she had always suspected but never quite been able to prove.

Her hand moved without thinking. She clicked **Print**.

Down the hall, the soft mechanical whir of the printer hummed to life, slicing through the silence like a blade.

She rose to her feet and walked slowly to the printer tray, each step deliberate, almost reverent.

She pulled the paper from the tray—just three pages, but they might as well have been granite. Stone carved with proof.

Truth.

She took the pages back to the living room and slid them into a manila folder already marked in her clean, deliberate handwriting:

"*Truth, In Her Own Words – Hard Copies*"

The folder was thick now. Each document a fragment of the story she never wanted to tell, but had no choice but to finish.

She held the folder against her chest for a moment, her heart pounding beneath it.

And then, to no one but herself, to the cat still asleep at her feet, to the midnight stillness surrounding her, she whispered:

"*You're going to lose, Valerie. Not because I'm smarter. But because I'm honest.*"

It wasn't a boast. It was a promise. A vow made in the dark, carried on the weight of two years' worth of pain, gaslighting, and financial ruin.

Sable stirred slightly at the sound of her voice but didn't wake.

The house remained still.

Celeste placed the folder back into the file box and pushed it slightly under the side table. Her hands trembled—not with fear this time, but with adrenaline. With purpose.

The tide had shifted. And she knew it.

There was still a war ahead. Deposition traps. Public scrutiny. More money hemorrhaging from her savings account with every passing hour.

But truth was a quiet weapon. And finally, it was hers to wield.

She turned off the lamp beside her, slid the laptop shut, and exhaled slowly.

Tomorrow, they would sharpen the blade.

But tonight, she let the weight of the moment settle around her like armor.

For the first time in a long time, she slept.

―――――――

CHAPTER TWELVE

DAY OF RECKONING

*"For what does it profit a man to gain the whole world, and
forfeit his soul?"*
— Mark 8:36 (ESV)

The sun hadn't fully risen yet, but the city was already
humming. Birds trilled in half-hearted bursts above the
concrete while traffic crawled around the courthouse steps like
it had somewhere more important to be.

Celeste stepped out of her car and straightened her coat. She
was wearing black—sleek, quiet, without ornament. The hem
of her wool skirt brushed against her calves in the chilly
morning wind. She pulled her collar higher, glancing down at
the fine gray hairs still clinging to the sleeve.

Sable.

Celeste didn't brush them off.

Jason rounded the front of the car. His steel-toe boots hit the pavement with dull weight, worn from a job site he'd left early just to be here.

"*Hold still,*" he said gently, smoothing her lapel, then tucked one rogue curl behind her ear. "*You got sleep?*"

Celeste gave the ghost of a smile. "*Four hours. Maybe five.*"

Jason exhaled hard and reached for her hand, squeezing it like a lifeline. His calluses were familiar now. Comforting. Real.

"*You're not walking in there alone.*"

"*I know,*" she whispered. But the truth was, she felt like she was.

The courthouse loomed before her like a monument to everything she'd lost. Three years of legal filings. Three years of subpoenas. Three years of silence and betrayal.

And today—*today*—would be the reckoning.

She looked at the building one last time, nodded once, and stepped forward.

––––––––

The air buzzed with tension. Court staff moved efficiently, their heels echoing against polished floors. Lawyers passed in murmured strategy. Security nodded absently at familiar faces.

But Celeste barely noticed. The moment she crossed into the building, the world narrowed.

Courtroom 2B.

She walked through the heavy oak doors with Croft beside her, Dana and Jason just behind. They'd agreed on no theatrics—no entourage, no makeup artists, no PR spin. Just truth.

Damien was already seated near the front, flanked by his new firm's legal team. When he turned and met her eyes, he didn't smile. He just nodded—low, somber, respectful. As if to say *We both survived her.*

Celeste gave him the same nod in return. No anger. Just quiet acknowledgment.

A soft rustle stirred as someone else entered. All heads turned.

Valerie.

She walked in with purpose, her soft white suit crisp and flawlessly tailored. She held her chin high, but her eyes betrayed the cost. The bravado was mechanical now. Practiced. Shaky.

Her attorney—a younger man with thinning hair and a voice that cracked when under pressure—walked slightly behind her, flipping through a binder he'd probably studied overnight. Valerie scanned the room quickly.

No Nathan.

Celeste watched her pause, just for a moment, when she realized it. Valerie's throat bobbed as she swallowed something bitter. Then she pushed forward and took her seat.

Croft leaned in toward Celeste, his voice low and calm.

"Today, it changes."

Celeste didn't answer right away. Her heart was pounding—not from fear, but from fatigue so deep it had fused into her bones.

"I'm not here to win," she said softly. *"I'm here to end it."*
Croft studied her a moment, then gave a single nod. Dana placed a hand briefly on Celeste's shoulder.

From the bench, the judge entered. Everyone rose.

Celeste's eyes didn't leave Valerie as they stood.

Valerie, obviously perturbed, didn't meet them.

———————

The bailiff called the room to order.

Opening statements would start soon. Croft adjusted his tie, Dana checked her notes. Across the aisle, Valerie's attorney whispered something in her ear. She nodded too quickly, lips drawn tight, eyes flicking from Celeste to the judge to the empty front row where Nathan should've been sitting.

The air in the courtroom thickened. Heavy. Anticipatory.
This wasn't a trial for money. This was the reckoning of a woman's soul.

Celeste kept her hands folded neatly in her lap.

As the judge cleared his throat and began to speak, she leaned forward slightly, ready—at long last—not to fight, but to finish.

COURTROOM, LATE MORNING

The hum of overhead lights buzzed faintly above the silence in Courtroom 2B. It was the kind of silence that held breath— thick, waiting, sharp.

Valerie Henshaw sat upright in the witness box, her hands folded tightly on her lap. The navy suit she'd worn that morning looked stiffer now, like armor that had begun to crack at the seams. She adjusted the microphone slowly and cleared her throat.

Croft stood just a few feet away, notes in hand, his expression unreadable.

"*Mrs. Henshaw,*" he began smoothly, "*you've testified under oath that your interactions with Ms. Monroe were professional. That you had no personal animus. That your only concern was workplace dynamics. Is that correct?*"

Valerie nodded. "*Yes, that's correct.*"

"And you maintain that the complaint you filed against her was accurate?"

"Yes."

"No exaggerations?"

She hesitated. *"No intentional ones."*

Croft's eyebrow twitched, almost imperceptibly. *"No intentional ones,"* he echoed. *"Let's explore that."*

He turned to the screen behind him, gesturing toward the monitor set up for exhibits.

"Exhibit 41C," he said.

On the screen appeared a printed email thread, time-stamped and sourced from Valerie's corporate account.

The subject line read: **RE: Notes on Celeste.**

Croft read aloud in an even tone, *"'We'll frame it like Celeste was disruptive. Get ahead of her.'"*

There was an audible shift in the courtroom. Chairs creaked. Someone sucked in a sharp breath.

Celeste didn't move. She didn't blink.

Valerie stared at the screen like it had betrayed her. Her throat bobbed.

"*That... that was taken out of context,*" she said.

Croft turned slowly. "*Let's give it context, then.*" He walked toward the witness stand and held up the printed thread.

"*This email was sent to Ms. Lisa Ayers, correct? Your then— HR manager.*"

Valerie nodded slowly.

"*And you say 'we'll frame it like Celeste was disruptive.' Not Celeste was disruptive—but we'll frame it. That phrasing, Mrs. Henshaw, suggests strategy, not observation. Doesn't it?*"

Valerie's lips parted. Her eyes darted briefly to her attorney, who said nothing.

"*I was worried about how her behavior might be perceived by others,*" she said finally. "*It was... a poor choice of words.*"

Croft didn't flinch. "*A poor choice of words. And yet it resulted in a multi-month record being built against my client. Formal documentation. Loss of opportunities. Internal notations. All under your advisement. All targeting Ms. Monroe.*"

Valerie's mouth pressed into a hard line. "*It wasn't personal.*"

"*No?*" Croft stepped aside, letting the screen switch to a second document.

"*Exhibit 43A. Internal Slack messages obtained via subpoena.*"

The courtroom screen now displayed an internal chat thread between Valerie and Lisa Ayers, dated months before any formal complaint had been made.

Croft read again, this time with deliberate emphasis.

> **VALERIE:** She's too sharp. Too confident. That can be dangerous.
> **LISA:** You mean Celeste?
> **VALERIE:** Yes. Watch her. We can't have her getting too comfortable.

The judge adjusted his glasses, leaned forward.

Valerie went pale.

"That wasn't... it wasn't meant like that," she said quickly. *"That was about team cohesion. About perception."*

Croft gave a small nod, almost thoughtful. *"Interesting, considering your previous testimony that there were no issues with team cohesion until after your complaint was filed."*

He turned to the judge. *"Your Honor, at this time, we'd like to call a supplemental witness to clarify the record: Lisa Ayers."*

The screen flickered, and then Lisa appeared via live video feed. She sat in what looked like a home office, backlit by sunlight, her posture stiff.

"Ms. Ayers," Croft began, *"can you state your name and position for the record?"*

"Lisa Ayers. Former Human Resources Manager at APEX Logistics."

"Ms. Ayers, you were contacted several months ago regarding Ms. Monroe's counterclaim. At the time, you declined to provide a sworn statement. What changed?"

Lisa looked straight into the camera. Her voice trembled, but her words were clear.

"I kept quiet because I didn't want to lose my job—or get involved in something this messy," she said. *"But I was part of something wrong, and I can't... I can't keep lying by omission."*

Croft nodded gently. *"Did Valerie Henshaw instruct you to begin documentation efforts against Ms. Monroe?"*

Lisa swallowed. *"Yes."*

"Did she express a desire to remove Ms. Monroe from the team?"

"Yes."

"Was there ever, in your professional opinion, a legitimate HR violation on Ms. Monroe's part?"

Lisa shook her head. *"No. Not that I ever observed or documented independently."*

The courtroom was dead silent. Even Valerie's attorney looked frozen.

Croft turned back to Valerie. *"Would you like to respond, Mrs. Henshaw?"*

Valerie looked like she might faint. Her face had gone waxy. Her voice, when it finally came, was hoarse.

"I didn't think it would go this far."

Croft's voice was quieter now, but sharper than ever.

"That's exactly the problem, Mrs. Henshaw. You never thought it would go this far—because you assumed no one would hold you accountable."

Croft flips to a new exhibit in his binder. The room stills again.

"Let's talk about Damien Carter," he says, slowly. *"The man you claimed to have seen breaking into a construction site late one evening."*

Valerie stiffens. *"Yes. I remember that night."*

Croft nods, eyes unreadable. *"So do we. Because your testimony formed the basis of internal allegations that nearly destroyed his career—and launched the defamation suit that dragged Ms. Monroe into this mess."*

He clicks a remote. On the screen appears a system log, projected for the courtroom.

"This is a full security audit from the Willow Creek development building, dated the night in question. No alarms

were triggered. No forced entry recorded. Surveillance footage from both interior and exterior cameras shows no unauthorized access. No Damien Carter. No break-in. Nothing."

Valerie opens her mouth, but Croft cuts in. "*Furthermore, an independent forensic review confirms that Mr. Carter's digital credentials—his badge number, login ID—were remotely manipulated. By an administrator-level account.*"

He lets the words sink in.

"*We traced the IP address used to execute the changes. It was registered to your home network, Mrs. Henshaw.*"

A shocked murmur ripples across the courtroom.

Valerie's voice cracks. "*That's not—I didn't—*"

Croft lifts a hand.

"*And here,*" he continues, sliding another document to the judge and clerk, "*is a message sent to Ms. Monroe three days later. A script. You fed her the story you wanted her to believe.*"

He reads aloud:

> "*You probably saved us from a major incident. Thank you for backing me up. This could've gone really badly if Damien hadn't been stopped.*"

Dana, beside Celeste, gasps softly.

Croft levels his gaze. *"There was no break-in. No crime. Just a fabricated narrative to redirect suspicion from yourself—and weaponize Ms. Monroe's trust."*

From her seat, Celeste sat completely still, her eyes locked on Valerie.

She should've felt something like victory. Some sliver of vindication.

But all she felt was *loss.*

This—this courtroom, this moment, this unmasking—was not a resurrection. It was a burial. Of five years of friendship. Of trust. Of identity. She looked at Valerie and saw not a villain, but a woman crumbling under the weight of her own lies. And it was devastating.

Dana leaned over and placed a folder in front of her. *"We're almost there,"* she whispered.

Celeste nodded—but her heart felt like it was being slowly unraveled.

Truth had come to light. But at what cost?

———

The door to the judge's chambers opened with a soft click, and all movement in the courtroom stilled as Judge Ralph Sampson emerged, his black robe flowing behind him like a final act curtain. The bailiff called the court to order with measured authority, though his voice held the fatigue of a long day.

Celeste's fingers were locked together in her lap, pale and stiff from tension. She hadn't moved since Valerie had stepped down from the witness box earlier, and now her back ached from sitting so still, so upright, for so long. But she didn't shift. She barely breathed.

To her right, Croft sat composed, his reading glasses perched low on his nose, hands folded neatly atop his legal pad. Dana stared at the bench, lips tight, almost daring the judge to disappoint her.

On Celeste's left, the chair Jason had occupied earlier sat empty. He'd needed to return to work after the lunch recess, though he'd promised to come back the moment the ruling was done. *"Text me the second it's over,"* he had said.

She wished he were here now. Not for answers, but for anchoring.

Across the aisle, Valerie sat again at the plaintiff's table. Her lawyer murmured something to her, but she gave no sign of hearing. Her eyes were fixed on the judge, and her mouth moved ever so slightly—silent, desperate prayers falling into the heavy air. Celeste noticed, vaguely, that Valerie's eyeliner had smudged again. That her blazer had a wrinkle that hadn't been there this morning. That she looked... smaller now. Folded inward.

Judge Sampson adjusted his notes and looked out over the room. His face was unreadable, voice steady.

"In the matter of Carter v. APEX Logistics, Celeste Monroe, concerning the claim of defamation and wrongful accusation," he began, and Celeste's entire body went taut.

Every hair on her arms lifted.

"...this court finds in favor of the defendant, Ms. Monroe."

A breath exhaled—Dana's. Croft placed a steadying hand on Celeste's shoulder, firm and quiet.

Celeste didn't move. Couldn't. For a second, the words didn't land. Then they did, all at once, like a tidal wave she'd braced against for months finally choosing to recede.

She blinked hard, her throat tightening. Her name had been cleared.

Damien's name had been cleared.

Three years of public suspicion. Rumors. Frozen smiles in meetings. Invitations rescinded. References lost. The sting of looking into her own reflection and wondering if *they* had gotten in her head—if the lie had taken root.

And now, in one breath, the court had finally said: *No. You were not wrong.*

A small, dry sound escaped her chest. Not quite a sob. More like a sigh collapsing into itself.

"Let the record show that this court recognizes no misconduct on Ms. Monroe's part," the judge continued. *"The allegations levied against her were found to be unsupported by the evidence, and no credible documentation or testimony has established her involvement in any wrongdoing. The court finds that Ms. Monroe was falsely implicated in a narrative orchestrated without basis in fact."*

There it was. The words she'd craved. Not vengeance—just truth. Just that.

She wanted to smile. She wanted to sob. She wanted to scream and shout and collapse into Jason's arms. But she just sat there. Hollow and stunned. Like someone who'd crawled across a battlefield and arrived at a flag that no longer mattered.

Judge Sampson continued, flipping to a second set of notes.

"In the matter of Monroe v. Henshaw, regarding counterclaims of fraud, intentional infliction of emotional distress, and malicious prosecution..."

The tone shifted. Subtly, but decisively.

Celeste's breath caught. Croft's hand lifted from her shoulder.

"...this court does not find sufficient evidence of malicious intent, nor does it find the burden of proof met regarding quantifiable emotional or financial damages that rise to the

level necessary for civil penalty under state statute. Motion denied. The plaintiff assumes all legal fees."

A long pause.

"The counterclaim is denied."

Silence.

Then—a gasp. Low and stunned—from the back row. Celeste didn't turn to see who it came from.

Dana's mouth parted. Her brows lifted in disbelief.

Croft inhaled quietly, lips pursing, as if he had anticipated the possibility but hoped—genuinely, deeply—that this wouldn't be how it ended.

Celeste blinked again. Once. Twice. Her mouth opened, then closed.

What?

The word didn't form aloud, but it thundered in her chest.

What do you mean denied?

Three years of unwarranted stress, $312,419 in fees, attorney bills, evidence. Missed holidays. Sleepless nights. Her reputation dragged through mud. Her career paused. The weight she'd carried and the weight she lost while trying to prove something she *knew* to be true.

And now—denied.

Valerie sat frozen, her mouth slightly ajar, as though she too wasn't sure what to make of the moment. She'd lost the case—but now escaped the financial consequences. Celeste could see it in her eyes: the dawning realization that she might walk out of this with nothing more than a bruised ego.

Judge Sampson concluded his statement.

"This matter is now closed. The court stands adjourned."

The gavel came down with a dull thud.

Croft reached for Celeste's bag, offering it to her like a gentleman escorting her from a wake. Dana stayed seated a moment longer, brows still furrowed, the legal mind inside her whirring even as the ruling settled into stone.

Celeste stood. Her legs were unsteady. Her vision blurred at the edges.

No victory speech. No champagne. Just the aching clarity of survival. She had won—but she was walking away with empty hands.

Croft looked at her gently. *"You cleared your name,"* he said, his voice low. *"That's not nothing."*

She nodded. Then shook her head.

"No," she whispered. *"It's not nothing. But it's not... enough."*

The courtroom doors creaked open behind Celeste, but she didn't turn. She didn't need to. She already knew who was leaving.

Valerie's seat was empty for the moment. Celeste could almost feel her absence, like a heavy presence lingering over her shoulder. The cold space where she'd sat for hours now throbbed with unspoken things—accusation, humiliation, the desperate silence of someone finally losing control.

Down the marble corridor, Valerie walked fast. Too fast. Her heels clacked in chaotic rhythm, echoing across the courthouse like a woman trying to outrun gravity. Her attorney struggled to keep pace, saying something she didn't hear. Or didn't care to.

As she neared the main exit, a cluster of reporters began to surge forward.

"Mrs. Henshaw, do you have any comment on the court's ruling?"

"Were you aware the messages would be introduced today?"

"Did you falsify records against Ms. Monroe?"

Valerie kept her head down, a tight grip on her handbag as though it might anchor her to some last scrap of dignity. Her jaw clenched. She didn't answer. Didn't blink. Didn't breathe until she shoved through the doors and into the late afternoon sun.

The SUV was waiting—Nathan's Escalade, the same one she'd insisted on keeping clean and immaculate. Today, it looked too polished, too big. Too indifferent. She yanked the door open and ducked inside, slamming it behind her as if to shut out the world itself.

Silence.

The leather smelled like vanilla and pine, but it didn't comfort her. Her phone buzzed in her coat pocket. Twice. Then a third time.

She pulled it out with trembling fingers.

Voicemail. Pastor Melvin.

She played it.

> *"Valerie... I'm praying for you. The truth has a way of surfacing, and we must answer for our choices. If you need to talk, I'm here. But this—this is between you and God now."*

She ended it before it finished.

Another notification lit up.

> **Email from:** *Office of General Counsel*
> **Subject:** *Internal Status Review*
> **Body Preview:** *"Your employment status is currently under review pending additional internal findings*

related to today's public disclosures. Further instruction to follow."

Her stomach dropped. She didn't open it.

The tinted window beside her caught her reflection—harsh and unforgiving. Mascara streaked beneath both eyes. Her lips were cracked. Hair flattened. Her mouth twisted at the sight of herself, but she didn't look away.

This is who she was now.

Not the polished mentor. Not the strategic genius in the corner office. Not the composed friend in the scripture-laced text threads. Just Valerie. And the wreckage.

She blinked slowly, still staring at herself, and whispered the only truth that came.

"You gained the whole world... and lost everything that mattered."

The SUV pulled away from the curb. Valerie didn't give her nephew any direction. She didn't have anywhere to go.

The glow of the fireplace flickered against the dark windows of Celeste's living room, casting long, quiet shadows across the hardwood floor. She stood in her kitchen, unmoving, one hand on the counter, the other hanging limp at her side. The house was still, heavy with the kind of silence that feels earned.

Sable wound herself around Celeste's ankle, brushing her soft fur in figure eights, persistent and comforting. Celeste glanced down, offered a tired smile, and reached to scoop the cat into her arms.

The front door knocked once—gentle, patient. She knew who it was.

She padded barefoot across the floor and opened the door.

Jason stood under the porch light, his coat damp from the misty night. His eyes scanned hers—reddened, swollen, rimmed with the exhaustion that no amount of sleep could fix.

He didn't say a word. He stepped inside and wrapped his arms around her.

Celeste leaned into him without resistance. Her face pressed into his shoulder as if she'd been holding her breath for months and could finally exhale.

"*I'm so sorry,*" he whispered.

"*It's okay,*" she murmured, though they both knew it wasn't. Then softer: "*I didn't do this to win money. I just... didn't want to be silenced anymore.*"

Jason pulled back just enough to meet her gaze. His voice was low, reverent, as if speaking to something holy.

"*You weren't. And you never will be again.*"

She nodded once, then pulled away gently. The grief wasn't sharp—it was worn down now, like stone smoothed by water. She moved with quiet intention, as if her body already knew what came next.

From the dining table, she picked up a portable filing case labeled in her own looping handwriting: *Thirty Pieces*

Inside: emails, deposition transcripts, highlighted lies, timelines—her war chest. The evidence she'd built over the three years. Each page had once felt like a sword. Now, felt like a weight she no longer needed to carry.

She crossed to the fireplace and knelt. The flames danced, alive and waiting.

With Jason watching silently from the sofa, Celeste slid the first page into the fire. The paper curled, blackened, dissolved. She fed it another. Then another.

She wasn't angry. She wasn't seeking vengeance.

She was letting go.

Because no matter how many people believed her now, no matter how publicly Valerie fell, the years had taken something from her that couldn't be restored in court.

She burned the paper that held Valerie's message to HR— *"We'll frame it like Celeste was disruptive."*

She burned the letter her lawyer wrote in response to her original request for information.

She burned the last printed screen of testimony from the HR witness who had waited too long to speak.

And when it was done, she sat back, her palms resting on her thighs, and watched the ashes collapse inward.

The silence settled again, warm and final. The house didn't feel like a battleground anymore. It felt like a home.

Sable pawed at her leg once and then settled down beside her, eyes blinking slowly. Jason hadn't moved. He knew this was hers to finish.

And then—*finally*—she wept.

There in the living room. Quiet, but raw. The kind of tears that come when the body can't hold the weight any longer.

They weren't tears of loss, or guilt, or fear.

They were tears for what justice didn't heal.

CHAPTER THIRTEEN

THIRTY PIECES

*"Then Judas threw the silver coins down in the Temple and
went out and hanged himself."*
— Matthew 27:5 (NLT)

CELESTE'S HOME OFFICE, A FEW HOURS BEFORE TRIAL

The late afternoon sun softly filters through the blinds, casting
narrow bands of light over the papers strewn across Celeste's
desk. She's been at this for hours, pushing through the
final stages of case prep. The weight of the last nearly three
years is pressing in on her—papers, digital files, the endless
details. She doesn't want to face it, but it's all there. A last
push before she can finally move on.

Celeste sits back in her chair, exhausted. She swipes through
her inbox, looking for an email she meant to review earlier.
Most of it is legal correspondence, updates, documents from
Croft's team. But then, one name catches her eye.

Valerie Henshaw.

It's a forwarded message from months ago. The subject line reads *Q4 Transition Planning.* Something about the subject doesn't sit right with Celeste. She clicks it open instinctively, as if drawn by some unseen force.

The file is an innocuous-looking Excel spreadsheet, all neat columns and rows. She starts scrolling through it, her eyes scanning for any familiar terms. The first few rows are company-related projections—budget estimates for the coming year, sales goals, internal restructuring. But then—something catches her breath.

The second tab is labeled *Post-litigation reintegration.*

Celeste's heart skips a beat. *Post-litigation?* She hesitates for a moment before opening the tab.

What she sees makes her fingers freeze on the keys.

The file lays out a series of detailed steps, like a blueprint for Valerie's future. The first row reads: *Media Coaching*—with notes on the type of press she would need after a loss. Beneath it, there's an itemized cost for *"narrative rebuilding."*

Celeste's stomach drops.

There's more: *Projected Legal Retainer.* She recognizes the name of the attorney firm listed—Valerie's own counsel. A retainer estimate, too, set at over half a million dollars. Beneath that: *Severance Simulation (if Monroe folds).*

Celeste's hands are shaking now, her pulse thudding in her ears as she scrolls. Her eyes track the numbers on the spreadsheet—projected costs, strategy for a clean exit.

She exhales, each breath getting heavier, more labored. Then, her gaze lands on a line near the bottom of the sheet:

"Net Profit (if successful claim against Monroe): $1,327,200."

The words seem to blur as her vision narrows, but she reads them again. Slowly. Carefully.

One million three hundred twenty-seven thousand two hundred dollars.

She leans back in her chair, staring at the screen. She can't breathe. The numbers are a cold, calculated evaluation of her life. *Her* future. Valerie had planned it all—the legal fees, the media campaign, the financial fallout that Celeste would be left to deal with.

But the final line—*Net Profit*—that was the punch in the gut. It wasn't just a defense strategy. It was a premeditated scheme. Valerie had bet everything on Celeste's downfall, her silence, her defeat.

Celeste blinks, and a sick, almost involuntary laugh escapes her lips.

This had been Valerie's plan. All along. She'd used the lawsuit, the legal wrangling, everything to secure a way out—a way to save her own career. Her future. And if Celeste had just folded, just walked away, it would have been enough. She would have gotten her prize: a financial windfall and freedom from the mess she created.

Valerie's *"thirty pieces"* weren't just money. They were her escape route—*her way out.* A backdoor for herself while dragging Celeste down.

A flash of clarity cuts through Celeste. It's like a switch flipping in her mind.

All this time, she'd thought the battle was about reputation—about proving her innocence. But it wasn't. It was about power. It was about control. Valerie had been playing her, pretending to be the ally when all along, Celeste had been nothing more than a pawn in a larger game.

This was never about me. Celeste stares at the screen. *This was never about me at all.*

She sits in silence for a long moment, letting the weight of it settle in her chest. There's no anger. No need for a final confrontation. Just a grim recognition that Valerie's betrayal was far deeper, far more intentional than Celeste could have ever imagined.

Celeste pulls her chair forward and drags the mouse to the file's corner. She clicks to close the spreadsheet, but the image of those numbers lingers in her mind. Slowly, she gathers the papers in front of her—the ones she's been reviewing for the case, the ones that have consumed her thoughts for nearly three years—and begins to organize them, a strange calm washing over her as she sets things in order.

This battle might be coming to an end, but what does it even matter now?

As Celeste closes her laptop, she catches her reflection in the window. Her face looks exhausted, but there's something different about it now. She's been through hell and back, but the clarity that comes from seeing the truth—it cuts through everything.

She wasn't the only one who had lost herself in this.

And for the first time, she understands: it wasn't just Valerie who needed redemption. It was her, too.

———

PRESENT DAY

The sun is dipping low, casting a warm, golden hue over the porch. A light breeze rustles the trees in the yard, and the scent of fresh-cut grass drifts in the air. It's the kind of evening where the world seems to pause—quiet, peaceful, like it's holding its breath. Celeste sits on the edge of the porch, her feet tucked under her, staring out at the quiet street. The weight of everything still lingers on her shoulders, even though the case is over, the battle won.

Jason steps out onto the porch, carrying two mugs of tea. He sits down beside her without a word, the soft clink of the mugs the only sound as he settles in next to her. There's a calmness in his presence that she's come to rely on. He doesn't ask if she's okay. He doesn't need to. The tea is a gesture of quiet support.

For a few moments, neither of them speaks. The only sound is the wind moving through the trees, the soft clinking of ice in the tea, the distant hum of traffic. It's as if Celeste is waiting for the right moment, waiting for the weight of it all to settle.

Finally, her voice breaks the stillness. It's flat, emotionless, but underneath the calm, there's a quiet storm swirling.

"She had a whole map for what her life would look like... if I lost," Celeste says, her eyes focused on the cup in her hands. Her fingers tighten around the handle, and she stares at the faint ripples in the tea. *"All those numbers. Those projections. It was like she had already written off me—written off everything about me."*

Jason doesn't say anything at first. He just listens. His eyes steady on her, taking in every word. He understands that this is the part where she needs to speak, to let it out.

Celeste continues, her voice soft but tinged with disbelief. *"A 'severance simulation,' she called it. Like I was just a number in her game. A way to secure her own... her own future."* She shakes her head, disbelief still fighting with the bitter taste of betrayal. *"I thought she was my friend. I thought—"* She stops herself, exhaling a long breath, *"I wanted to believe she was my friend. I needed to believe it. That's the worst part."*

The words hang in the air between them, thick with the weight of everything that has happened. Jason takes a slow sip of his tea, his expression steady, but there's a warmth in his eyes when he looks at her.

"No," he says softly. *"The worst part would've been letting that lie stay true."*

Celeste looks at him, her gaze sharp. She's surprised, but in that way that feels like the clarity of truth finally cutting through. Jason's words are simple, but they carry a depth of understanding she hasn't realized she needed until now.

"What do you mean?" she asks, her voice quiet, almost uncertain.

Jason sets his cup down, his focus entirely on her now. He turns his body toward hers, his presence steady and solid beside her. *"The worst part would've been if you had let that lie control you. If you had let her manipulate you into believing that what she wanted was more important than what you needed. That's where she would've won."*

Celeste's eyes search his face, the quiet intensity in his words washing over her. He's right. She had needed to believe Valerie was her friend. The weight of that belief had kept her grounded in the storm—until it all shattered. But Jason's words remind her that *she didn't let it destroy her.* In the end, she didn't allow Valerie's lies to break her.

For a long moment, Celeste simply stares at him. She's so used to carrying everything alone, to being the one who holds it all together, but right now, in this quiet, golden moment, she feels the space between them fill with something else—trust. Not just in the quiet support he gives, but in herself, too.

She leans back slightly, resting her shoulders against the porch railing. "*I wanted to believe in her, Jason. I wanted so badly for her to be on my side.*" Her voice cracks slightly on the last word, and she swallows hard, fighting back the wave of emotion. It's not just about Valerie anymore—it's about everything Celeste had hoped for, everything she'd wanted to believe in her life. All the people who had let her down.

Jason watches her quietly, not rushing to fill the silence with words. He knows. He knows the depth of the battle she's fought, and he knows what it takes to let go.

"*I know,*" he says finally, his voice soft, but steady. "*And I think that's what makes this whole thing so hard. It wasn't just the betrayal. It was losing that part of you, too—the part that still wanted to believe in her. But you're here. You're still standing. You didn't lose yourself, Celeste. And that's what matters.*"

Celeste smiles faintly at his words, and it's not a triumphant smile, but something gentler—a recognition that the weight has lessened. She looks out at the street again, the amber light of the setting sun spilling across the pavement, and for a moment, she feels the quiet stillness of peace settle over her.

"*I didn't lose myself*," she repeats softly, almost to herself. There's a weight in those words, a finality that feels both like release and strength.

Jason doesn't say anything else for a while. He doesn't need to. The air between them is full of understanding. Celeste feels the coolness of the tea in her hands and the quietness of the evening settling in her chest. For the first time in a long time, she feels truly anchored.

"*You don't need to carry it all*," Jason says finally, his voice low, like a promise.

Celeste turns her head slowly, her gaze meeting his. The vulnerability in her eyes is palpable. "*I don't know if I can stop carrying it all.*"

"*You don't have to*," he replies softly. "*Not anymore. Not if you don't want to.*"

For a moment, they just sit together in silence, the soft clink of the tea mugs punctuating the stillness. Celeste closes her eyes for a brief second, taking in the weight of everything he's said. The hurt, the betrayal, the exhaustion—it all lingers, but it's not crushing her anymore. It's just... there. And that's okay.

She leans her head back, letting out a long, slow breath. "*I'm tired*," she says quietly.

Jason nods. "*I know.*"

And for the first time, in the quiet, golden light of the setting sun, Celeste allows herself to lean into that truth. That she's not alone. That she doesn't have to carry everything on her own.

The church is eerily quiet when Celeste steps inside, the heavy wooden doors creaking softly as they close behind her. The scent of old wood and incense lingers in the air, mingling with the faint trace of vanilla from the small sachets hanging in the rafters. The sanctuary, though small, is warm in its simplicity. Soft light filters in through the stained-glass windows, casting colorful patterns on the stone floor. The room feels alive with history, filled with silent echoes of prayers whispered over the years, but it's empty now.

Celeste stands for a moment in the doorway, feeling the weight of the quiet. It's a comfort, in a way. No eyes watching, no expectations—just space. Just silence. She breathes in deeply, her chest rising and falling with a slow, steady rhythm, as if the air here holds something she can't quite name.

Pastor Melvin isn't here. He was never someone Celeste felt deeply connected to, but the church had always been Valerie's refuge. It was where Celeste had gone when the world had felt too heavy to bear, when Valerie had invited her to seek solace during her own grief. Now, it feels like the place where so much began to fall apart.

Celeste walks quietly down the aisle, past the empty pews, and settles close to the back row, her favorite spot from the few times she'd come here. She lets her gaze fall on the empty altar, the worn cushions on the pews, the dim light casting long shadows on the walls. It's peaceful. But it's not the same.

For a moment, she simply sits there. The stillness is almost overwhelming. She closes her eyes, resting her hands in her lap, grounding herself in the quiet. The past feels far away in this moment—almost like another life. And yet, it lingers, just beneath the surface of her thoughts.

Celeste's mind drifts to the words of scripture Valerie had quoted to her so many times: *"All things work together for good."*

At the time, it had been an easy mantra, something that felt like an assurance from God. It had given Celeste hope, made her believe that even in the midst of suffering, things would work out for the best. But now? Now, the words ring hollow. Or maybe they're truer than ever. The irony isn't lost on her: Valerie had said them as if to shield herself from guilt, from the cost of the lies she had woven. But for Celeste, the truth had brought something far more painful: clarity. And in the midst of that clarity, the words suddenly feel more like an affirmation of what *was*—that all things have worked together, indeed. But not in the way Valerie intended.

Celeste exhales slowly. She doesn't pray aloud. There are no pleas or requests, no demands for answers. Just quiet. Just breathing.

Her thoughts drift to Valerie—how she must be faring now. Valerie had lost everything. Nathan had moved out with

Madison weeks ago, filing for divorce shortly after the verdict. The weight of it all had come down on Valerie in a rush—her career crumbling, her family falling apart, her church family distancing itself from her. She had walked away from everything, retreating into the silence she had created with her lies.

Celeste didn't feel sorry for her. But there was something in the quiet that made her think of the profound loss Valerie had suffered. Not just in the material sense, but in her soul—her faith, her family, her relationships. Everything she had built to preserve her own control had crumbled, piece by piece. Valerie had become a prisoner of her own machinations.

Celeste opens her journal, flipping to a fresh page. She reaches for the pen, her hand trembling just slightly as she begins to write. The words come slowly at first, like she's still not entirely sure what she wants to say, but the act of writing feels right. Feels necessary.

"I wasn't perfect. But I told the truth. And I'm still standing."

The words settle on the page, heavy with the weight of everything Celeste has been through. She isn't sure why she's writing them, but it feels important to acknowledge it. She *did* tell the truth. Even if it cost her everything. Even if it didn't bring the ultimate resolution she imagined. It cost her a lot—perhaps more than she'll ever fully understand—but the truth had been the only thing she had left.

She takes another deep breath, her mind wandering again to the story she thought she knew about Valerie. To the woman who had once stood beside her, the woman she had once trusted. She hadn't been perfect either—Celeste knew that. But she had done her best, and in the end, that was all she could have done.

Celeste closes the journal, the words written now a small comfort. A declaration of her own strength, of her own survival.

But before she leaves, she stands and walks slowly toward the altar. There, on the edge, is a small votive candle, the faint glow beckoning her. Celeste pauses, her hand hovering over the flame, and then, without hesitation, she lights the candle. The soft flicker of the fire dances in the quiet sanctuary, casting a warm light on her face.

She whispers the words, almost too softly to hear, but they feel right, like something she has been carrying for too long is finally being released.

"Forgive her, Lord. But don't let me forget."

The words are both a prayer and a promise. Forgiveness doesn't mean forgetting, Celeste knows that now. It doesn't mean erasing the hurt, erasing the pain. But forgiveness is *necessary*—for her, for her peace. For Valerie, maybe, too. But not for *her* forgetting.

Celeste stands for a moment longer, watching the candle burn in silence. It's small. Quiet. But somehow, it feels like a powerful act of closure. A mark on the page of this chapter, where the book finally closes.

As she turns to leave, she feels something shift within her—a lightness. Not from the weight of forgiveness, but from the quiet acceptance of what happened, what was lost, and what can never be undone.

She walks out of the sanctuary, the quiet stillness of the church following her.

The neighborhood is asleep.

Porch lights flicker like beacons across driveways, casting soft glows on trimmed hedges and silent sidewalks. Somewhere in the distance, a sprinkler kicks on with a soft hiss, then dies again. A breeze stirs the leaves overhead. It is the kind of night that asks nothing. The kind that simply *is*.

Celeste steps outside barefoot, a mug of lukewarm tea forgotten in her hand. She lowers herself onto the wide stone steps of her porch, exhaling slowly as she settles into the cool, quiet air. Her robe gathers around her ankles. The stones beneath her feet are cold, grounding. Her long curls are still damp from a late shower, sticking to her skin. But the night air feels good.

Sable slinks through the doorway behind her and hops down beside her, tail brushing lightly against her shin. The cat curls up with practiced ease, pressing her soft body against Celeste's side, like an anchor.

Overhead, the stars are out—scattered and still, blinking down like quiet witnesses. For the first time in what feels like years, Celeste doesn't feel watched. Not by lawyers. Not by Valerie. Not by whispers in the breakroom or red dots on her bank statement.

There's no verdict waiting.
No inbox full of subpoenas.
No curated narrative to unravel.

Just the stillness.
Just the stars.
Just *truth.*

She draws her knees up to her chest and wraps her arms around them. The world still spins in its chaos. She knows that. She knows someone else, somewhere else, is facing the kind of betrayal that leaves permanent bruises on the soul. She knows there are still women silenced, still people weaponizing faith and friendship and fear for personal gain. The machine hasn't stopped just because her trial ended.

But tonight, that machine can't touch her.

No one calls.
No reporters wait at the curb.
No promises of restitution come in tidy envelopes.

There is no parade.
No victory.
But also—no pretending.

And that, somehow, is enough.

Celeste closes her eyes and breathes in deep, letting the air stretch wide inside her chest before releasing it again. She looks up at the stars, and for a moment, she feels small in the best possible way.

This world is cruel sometimes—often, even.

But she isn't.

That's what mattered in the end.

She thinks of Valerie—not with venom, not with pity. Just... as someone who had a choice and made the wrong one. Valerie wanted control. She wanted leverage. An exit plan that used Celeste's silence as a launch pad.

But silence didn't win.

Truth did.
Not cleanly. Not without cost.
But it won.

Celeste presses her cheek to her knee, eyes drifting closed as she whispers to the night—not for anyone else, not even for Sable.

Just for herself.

"It cost me everything to tell the truth. But it cost Valerie even more to hide it."

The words slip into the air like smoke from a candle—soft and real and irreversible.

No thunder rolls. No tears fall.
Just the final, simple knowing that she endured.

And in that knowing, she finds peace.
Not the kind that erases what happened.
But the kind that says: *I lived through it. And I didn't become it.*

Inside, the house is still. The legal folders are gone. The fire has long since eaten the last page. Her savings account remains drained. Her career… uncertain. But her soul?

Intact.
Clear.
Unbroken.

She strokes Sable absently, and the cat lets out a quiet purr—content, safe.

The night holds its breath for a moment longer.

Then, softly, the final truth rises in Celeste's heart, as the stars blink quietly overhead.

Justice didn't heal her.
But it freed her.
And this time, she would never trade that for anything—
not even thirty pieces of silver.

In a world that profits off betrayal and spins silence into strategy, Celeste stood for something simple and rare: **truth**.

She didn't fight because she was flawless.
She fought because she refused to be complicit.

And in doing so, she reminded us—that the measure of a person is never in what they lose when they stand up, but in what they keep when everything else is stripped away.

Dignity.
Integrity.
Faith.
Decency.

In times like these, when the world feels wild and dark, those things are the real currency.

And they are always worth more than silver.

---

www.ingramcontent.com/pod-product-compliance
Lightning Source LLC
Chambersburg PA
CBHW031939010726
47493CB00007B/1998